I0602022

DAUGHTER OF SOULS & SILENCE

ROGUE ETHEREAL SERIES BOOK TWO

ANNIE ANDERSON

DAUGHTER of SOULS & SILENCE
Rogue Ethereal Book 2

International Bestselling Author
Annie Anderson

All rights reserved
Copyright © 2018 Annie Anderson
No part of this book may be reproduced, distributed, transmitted in
any form or by any means, or stored in a database retrieval system
without the prior written permission from the author. You must not
circulate this book in any format. Thank you for respecting the rights
of the author. This is a work of fiction. Names, characters,
businesses, organizations, places, events, and incidents are either the
products of the author's imagination or used in a fictitious manner.
Any resemblance to actual persons, living or dead, or actual events is
purely coincidental.

Edited by Angela Sanders
Cover Design by Tattered Quill Designs

www.annieande.com

For my baby sister - even though this isn't the book she wants me to write. Suck it up, buttercup. This is what you get.

BOOKS BY ANNIE ANDERSON

THE ARCANE SOULS WORLD

GRAVE TALKER SERIES

Dead to Me

Dead & Gone

Dead Calm

Dead Shift

Dead Ahead

Dead Wrong

Dead & Buried

SOUL READER SERIES

Night Watch

Death Watch

Grave Watch

THE WRONG WITCH SERIES

Spells & Slip-ups

Magic & Mayhem

THE ETHEREAL WORLD

PHOENIX RISING SERIES

(Formerly the Ashes to Ashes Series)

Flame Kissed

Death Kissed

Fate Kissed

Shade Kissed

Sight Kissed

ROGUE ETHEREAL SERIES

Woman of Blood & Bone

Daughter of Souls & Silence

Lady of Madness & Moonlight

Sister of Embers & Echoes

Priestess of Storms & Stone

Queen of Fate & Fire

"Hell is empty, and all the devils are here."

— WILLIAM SHAKESPEARE

MAX

There are some things I'd have hoped to never experience. Being eaten alive by carnivorous ants, missing a shoe sale, being forced to watch *Gomer Pyle* reruns—you know, the really evil stuff. There are other things I didn't even think to put on the list. Being dragged by the arm by a bitchy angel into a room full of Ethereal elders probably should have been at the tippy-top. Had I known it was a thing, I probably would have written it down or something, but alas...

"You know, that 'never harming the other side shit' goes both ways, Ruby," I warn my captor as she drags me through the hidden halls of a club the pair of us are very familiar with. Her definitely more than me.

One could say Aether was where everything started, and they'd be right, in a way. This underground witch club was my first real introduction to my kind in a very long time.

But they weren't all my kind, now were they? Witch DNA only accounted for half my makeup. The other half was a bag of cats even I didn't want to get in the middle of. And truth be told, if Ruby Sinclair wasn't dragging me through the place, I probably wouldn't even be allowed to grace these halls with my presence.

From what I'd gathered in the weeks following my parental reveal, demons weren't welcome most places. In my case, being half-demon made it so I wasn't welcome in my own family.

Go figure.

"Oh, please. It's no worse than you throwing me across the room, Max, and you know it," she snarls, which is a feat considering she's about as menacing as a tabby cat. Blonde hair, big boobs, porcelain skin. I had a feeling she wasn't *just* an angel. I also figured she was probably a bit more threatening to people who weren't me.

But Ruby had a point. I did toss her across the room like a rag doll, and keeping the smile off my face as I recall the memory is harder than I thought it would be.

"Yes, but you landed in a very comfy chair with exactly zero bruises, and that stunt helped suss out a black-market dealing asshole. This right here"—I return while tugging my upper arm out of her grip—"is just you being a dick."

More like it was her way to push the limit of the law as far as it would go. I couldn't harm her without starting an all-out angel-demon Armageddon. But then again, she couldn't harm me, either. I wonder how much leeway she could get, since she was essentially taking me to jail or to a judge, or whatever. All she'd said after she broke into my home was that she was taking me to the Council.

Not that I really knew what that meant.

"*Fine.*" Ruby turns down a hallway I'd yet to traverse. "Follow me and stay close. I don't have time to hunt you down if you decide to rabbit on me. I have shit to do."

What shit exactly *she* had to do, I had no idea. As far as I understood it, Ruby was Caim's bodyguard, bounty hunter, lap dog, and all-around gofer.

Rather than roll my eyes, I follow her down a shadowy hallway away from the revelers and music—away from the safety a crowd of that size provides—and step closer and closer to a place I have no desire to be.

They say I broke the law by killing Micah, the incubus who branded me. Maybe I did, but deciding between killing a man, or becoming a slave to him for the rest of my long life, well... it was really no decision.

Too bad I didn't read the fine print on the bone blade my mother gave me.

Ruby stops at a door that seems to have popped up out of nowhere. The wood is an ornately carved mahogany. In the dim, it takes me a minute to recognize the words etched into the frame. *Numera omnes qui ingrediuntur ad iudicium.*

Judgment comes to all who enter.

Well, that isn't ominous or anything.

Ruby's corn silk hair falls in a sheet down her back, highlighting when she fidgets, hesitating before opening the heavy door. Ruby doesn't fidget, and she doesn't hesitate. Not ever. Her pause causes the hair on the back of my neck to stand up, and I don't like it one bit.

She shoves it open, revealing a bright room, nearly blinding after immersing myself in the dark pockets of the nightclub. She steps aside, waiting for me to enter. Just like Caim's magical portal of an office—*which skeeves me the fuck out*—this room seems to be here, and then again *not* here. We've all done it—made a temporary portal when we don't want to bother with something so pedestrian as actual travel—but permanent portals like this one are on my long list of things that are probably not so good for the balance of magic.

I look back down the long hallway, catching glimpses

here and there of club-goers living it up, and I wonder if I'll ever be like them.

Carefree.

Accepted.

Doubtful.

"Any day now," Ruby gripes, and I have the distinct urge to put my fist in her face. I don't, but I really want to.

I heave a longsuffering sigh and step into the room. The snick of the latch closing just behind me does absolutely nothing to help my rising trepidation at what is a huge, honking unknown. Immediately, I feel underdressed. The space is wall-to-wall marble, the bright white of it threaded through with waves of gray. To my right is a room that seems to go on forever, the shadowless whiteness reaching on and on in a vastness that my eyes just can't seem to comprehend. To my left, is a raised dais with what seems to be a judge's bench.

Only there isn't just one judge.

There are eight seats, but only six are filled. Large expertly carved wooden thrones, each with a totem above the headrest. In the first seat is Caim, his blue eyes blazing as he grinds his teeth. He is a bit less poised than I'm used to, which doesn't spell good things. The totem on his seat is a pair of spread wings.

Next to him is a tiny, fine-boned blonde. On the

street, I wouldn't put her past thirty. On this dais, with her eyes assessing me in the way that they are, I'd say she was ancient. Her rosy lips quirk into a half-smile that isn't comforting at all. Her totem is a dragon, its mouth open in a snarl.

Beside her is a giant, thin in the extreme, his expressionless face seeming to see me and see through me all at the same time. His totem is an hourglass. Next to him is an open seat, the wood of the totem molded into the fluid form of a phoenix.

Down the line is a quite attractive but scowling man, his sable-brown hair brushed from his face in an artfully messy way that is made to look effortless, but in no way actually is. His totem is a pentagram. Next to him is my grandmother, Bernadette—or Lilith if we want to get technical. She's wearing a white suit jacket with pearls. I can't tell what is behind the bench, but I'd lay money on her being in a skirt. Her totem, frighteningly enough, is what appears to be a gargoyle's head, its mouth open in a screaming hiss, fangs bared, tongue lolling. But Bernadette's face is carefully blank.

Not good.

Beside her is a gruff-looking man with silver eyes and weathered skin, dressed in flannel and looking like he'd rather be drinking a beer at a pub than be within a hundred miles of here. His hair is long and shaggy, falling into his eyes. The hair on his chin is three days past scruff and entering scraggy-beard territory. His totem is a wolf baying at some unseen moon.

Next to him is the other empty chair, the totem on it a haunting version of *The Scream* only with less abstractness and too much abject realism.

Angel, dragon, warlock, phoenix, witch, demon, shifter, wraith. The heads of all the Ethereal factions sitting in one place. Well, almost all of them. I knew the two that were missing personally, but my "in" with the leaders of the phoenix and wraith faction would probably do little to help me now.

Especially since the remaining six—well, except for my gramma—were all staring at me like I was a puppy who shit on an heirloom rug.

Fuck a duck, I am screwed.

They don't start with pleasantries, no one introducing themselves to me or even attempting to be civil. The brown-haired witch snaps his fingers and a hard-backed wooden chair springs up out of nowhere. I assume he wants me to sit, but I ignore the chair out of spite and cross my arms, my bravado hopefully hiding that I feel mighty underdressed and at a loss. Had I known I was going to meet what was inherently Ethereal royalty, I would have at least done my hair.

As it stood, I was in black, skinny jeans with the

cuffs rolled up, electric-blue Converse, and a hot-pink semi-see-through tank that said "Adios Bitchachoes" with a lacy black bra underneath and a messy bun on top of my head. Yep. I probably should have asked Ruby for a timeout so I could at least put on something presentable.

Why didn't Bernadette tell me, warn me? Why didn't Caim? Did I mean so little to the both of them that they wouldn't give two shits about me sitting—well, standing —right where I am?

"Do you know why you're here?" the blonde dragon asks. Her accent is thick, maybe Russian or Ukrainian perhaps.

"I have an idea," I drawl, my left eyebrow hitching up without permission.

Oh, I have more than an idea. I know exactly why I'm here. It probably has something to do with the demon I killed.

"Good, then we'll dispense with the pleasantries. Maxima Alcado, born Maxima Christina Arcadios, Rogue witch, denounced member of the former Arcadios Coven, shunned daughter of the demon Andras and Pacific Northwest Coven leader, Teresa Alcado, sole heir to the royal seat, you are hereby accused of murdering your Master, Micah Goode, with a forbidden instrument."

A high-pitched buzzing takes over my hearing as a biting cold seems to seep into my limbs. I hate that name. Hate the way my body betrays me every single time I hear it. Both his name and the one I was given when I came into this world. *Arcadios.* I thought I'd buried that part of me just like my mother had. I guess not. And Micah's. I hate the way just the specter of him makes it so I can't go home, can't even look at my house without my breath coming in these same short pants of an impending panic attack.

It isn't fair. I didn't ask to be branded. I didn't ask to be born in the family I was. And that's why Micah wanted me. Because of who my family is. Because of the blood running in my veins.

I guess the self-defense excuse was probably moot here.

I open my mouth to say just that when I hear my gramma's voice in my head, her crisp English accent echoing through the edges of my brain.

Don't say a word, Maxima dear. I'll fix this. I swear to you. I'll fix this.

I meet her warm brown eyes, knowing she means it, but also knowing that if it came to it, I might be beyond saving.

"Have you nothing to say?" The witch's tone is snide as he sneers at me.

I shift my gaze from Bernadette to him, keeping my face impassive, looking him over. Yes, he's attractive, but his sneer sours his looks. My assessment must unnerve him because he shifts in his seat.

Probably used to a bit more groveling, I bet.

"So be it." He pauses—probably for effect—taking over the speaking for the dragon, a little upward crook of his mouth. "The sentence for your crimes is death. Do you have anything to say now?"

It turns out I didn't.

2

MAX

I feel a hysterical giggle bubbling up my chest as I utilize the wooden chair to take a load off. I'd stopped my bestest friend on this planet from killing one fucking demon—which prevented the Fate's forsaken Apocalypse, I might add—and this is the thanks I get?

A death sentence? Were they fucking high?

Bernadette's crisp voice echoes through my brain again, and I wonder if she'll teach me that trick in the few minutes I have left on this earth.

My guess is probably not.

I want you to remind them of a little thing called consent. It isn't just for prom dates, pumpkin. Even demons require it.

Consent. Is that going to be my saving grace?

"Really? A death sentence. And may I ask, can you prove that Micah was my master?" I question the silent panel of judges. "I don't think you can. Because I don't see any brands on my arms, and I know for a fact that his death would not erase them. If he were my master, then his death would have meant my own. And I'm still breathing," I snarl, my arms open wide to show them the smooth, tattooed skin.

"All I see are tattoos. Maybe you covered the brands." The witch's snide slips a bit when I call him on his bullshit. What am I, a rustler trying to cover up a horse brand?

"You know good and well I can't cover up those marks. You can't prove he was my master, can you? And if you can't prove it, then you can shove your death sentence up that tiny little pinprick you call an asshole." I'm addressing them all, but my eyes are focused on the witch who gained so much pleasure from announcing my death sentence and my Rogue status as if I was slime on his shoe. I get a little thrill when his face turns indignant as he sputters.

I don't think anyone has ever talked that way to him probably ever. I love being the first to do things.

That was not what I meant, Maxima, and you know it.

I shrug at her, giving an unrepentant smile.

It takes precisely two-point-five seconds to come to the realization that if they wanted to kill me, they would have done it already. There would be guards or something. My magic would have been suppressed.

I snap my fingers to test my theory, watching as the green of my power slides like a molten fire over my fingers. I snap them again and an ottoman springs up under my feet. I cross my ankles and my arms at the same time as I level them all with a hard expression.

I'm tired, I'm pissed. It's been a long day, and this bullshit isn't making it any better.

"There is also the issue of consent. Micah for damn sure didn't have it, and I was under the impression it was required for one to be enslaved for all of eternity. And you're telling me, he branded the next in line to the royal demon seat or whatever against her will, and I'm the one sentenced to die? As far as I'm concerned, the only one here who broke the law is Micah, and I cut out the middleman and took care of him for you. You're welcome. Can we just cut the shit already? You all want something from me. So instead of bullshitting me with this asinine death sentence that I know for a Fate's forsaken fact you will not carry out, why don't you just tell me what you want?"

What I'd really like to know is where exactly these

people were when Micah was off murdering humans and butchering his baby mama. I want to know where they were when he was trying to make me submit, when he was taking over my mind, when he was making me afraid of my own skin.

Sitting here up on high, I suspect.

Bernadette raises an eyebrow but can't hide the way her lips decide to curve up at the corners. A few months ago, I might have smiled with her, but today I've had about enough of this bullshit.

I'm missing my lesson with Ian for this malarkey. Ian. I hope he doesn't worry about me. That's a lie. I kind of hope he does a little, but not enough to cause real harm. I'm in that weird, selfish place where I want him to give a shit but don't want him to be inconvenienced.

Feelings are weird.

"We... You..." the witch sputters. *Oh, dear, I think I broke him.*

"What Barrett is trying to do even though he insofar has bungled it up royally, is to ask you for help. There was a vote earlier on how this would go because your grandmother suggested using fear as a motivating tactic would be unwise. The five remaining voted, and you can see how that's going," the shifter explains. "My name is

Marcus, by the way, and if you'd be so inclined to hear us, I'd like to ask you for a favor."

"This is *not* what we discussed!" Barrett hisses around my grandmother.

"And what was your threatening her going to do?" Marcus retorts. "Piss her off so she'll never help us? Were you going to attempt to kill her and then get your ass kicked by someone a quarter your age? Fear doesn't work on everyone, you know." I get stuck on the age thing. I'm nearly four hundred. That would mean Barrett is edging on twelve hundred. I've never met a witch over eight hundred.

Old as fuck or not, Barrett is still a dick. "She *broke* the law." If anything, he is persistent, and at this point, I wish I had popcorn because this is better than reality TV.

"No, she didn't. Micah did not have consent. Not only that, there is no way on any plane of existence Micah Goode should have ever tried to enslave a princess. And what are you defending him for?"

"I defend the law. No matter who breaks it, it is our job to uphold it. If there is no law, then there will only be chaos." Barrett bangs his fist on the bench like a gavel. "She killed the demon who branded her—with a forbidden weapon, no less—and you want to ask her for a favor? Are you getting senile in your old age, Marcus?"

Marcus rolls his eyes in a way that would make a teenager proud, turning his body back to me. "As you can see, we still have somewhat of a debate on the validity of your supposed breaking of the law."

"If we're getting technical, I've been a Rogue since I was fourteen. I don't know any of your laws, and as far as I can tell, you should be thanking me. Because if I didn't kill Micah, Striker Voss would have. Which if I recall correctly, would have started the fucking Apocalypse. *Again*, you're welcome."

This earns me a sharp stare from the dragon lady, and I have a hard time keeping my chuckle to myself. They have to tell me their names, so I'm not just thinking of them by their totems.

"Can you guys maybe introduce yourselves? I know Caim and Bernadette and now Barrett and Marcus, but the rest of you…" I trail off, shrugging in the hopes that they understand why I wouldn't know them. Being cast out of my family at such a young age means I know less than I probably should about this world. The warlock takes pity on me first.

"I am known as Gorgon, child," the warlock murmurs. Warlocks have always been very interesting to me, typically bald even as children no matter the sex, taller than even the tallest human, and thin in the extreme, warlocks aren't as mainstream as your average witch or shifter. In my four hundred years, I don't think I've seen even a handful, and their abilities are something out of a *Dr. Who* episode. Warlocks bend time to their will, shaping it and molding it to their needs. Or at least that's what I've heard. I'd never actually met one until today.

I give him my most polite smile. "Pleased to meet you, Mr. Gorgon." My impromptu manners must catch him by surprise because I get a shocked sort of laugh out of him.

"And I am Cinder," the dragon says, and something about the way she moves seems familiar somehow. I give her a nod in deference.

"Again, pleased to meet you all."

"I'm sorry about the circumstances, Max, but like Marcus said, we need a favor," Caim starts, and I swear I almost forgot the angel was here. "It isn't one we ask lightly, and it isn't one we want to ask at all. But there are only two people on this earth that can carry it out, and there is no way we could ask Bernadette to do it." His face is ravaged as if he in no way wants to ask what he's about to, and it's slowly killing him. Shit.

"There's a reason you are next in line for the royal seat even though you're a Rogue. Your father, Andras—"

"He might be my father by blood, but I don't know the man." I cut Caim off, rage tinting my vision red. I hate being associated with that man. I hate being associated with my parents at all. I don't know them, not really. The both of them abandoned me in their own way since birth. My father in all the ways that mattered, and my mother...

She might have birthed me, and she might have housed me for the first fourteen years of my life, but she never, not once, loved me.

"Be that as it may, he is your father, and the reason I'm in this seat right now is that he killed his brother, your uncle, Samael. He... murdered my youngest son," Bernadette admits, her voice breaking at that last bit as if the truth of it has just hit her.

Pain streaks across her face as she grits her teeth, and the toll all of this has taken on her starts to show. Her expression that was once so warm is now hollow with the ravages of grief.

"In light of the fact that you are probably the only being on this plane who could kill Andras, we are willing to pardon your murder charge and trust that you will use your weapon within the parameters set forth by this Council—if you dispatch him for us. Then, and only then, will you take your rightful seat," Barrett informs me, his bearing as if he's doing me a big favor.

"Let me see if I have this right. You want me to avenge the murder of a man I've never met by killing another man I've never met? And then join a Council I've never even heard of until a few months ago? Oh, and on top of that you will 'forgive' my self-defense against a woman-beating, black-market dealing sociopath who branded me against my will. Am I just supposed to roll over like a dog and say thank you, sir, I'll be sure to get right on that?"

"Andras killed your uncle," Barrett tosses back as if that means something.

"So? He's a man I have never met and didn't even know about until a minute ago. Maybe the politics of this world are a bit more important to you than they are to me. Did you seem to forget that I'm a Rogue? I have no family or a home or laws that protect me. As demonstrated by your bullshit murder charge."

"It won't just be your uncle he goes after, Maxima," Caim warns.

"You know, I think it's hilarious you have the gall to ask me for a favor when the last time I did you one it almost got me killed."

Caim rears back as if I'd slapped him, which is good because he deserves it.

I'm not a tool. I'm not a pawn. If they want something done, they'll just have to do it themselves.

Despite the grief I know Bernadette must feel, this is asking way too much.

"The answer is no."

3

MAX

My eyes barely adjust to the dim as I storm from what was likely my own personal band of executioners. No one is in the hallway when I emerge from the all-white high courtroom, which is a freaking boon in my book. Maybe that isn't what it is, but the bright, colorless room makes me think of the pearly gates they talk about in stories. I was seriously expecting Barrett to transform into Saint Peter somehow and punt my ass to Hell. I'm just happy Ruby isn't here. I would slap the taste out of her mouth, Apocalypse be damned. It isn't long before I'm outside Aether, breathing in great gulps of air as the panic that I managed to stave off hits me like a sledgehammer.

Ruby was in my home. She just walked right in

without so much as a blip. She found me—anyone could find me.

You weren't hiding, remember? You took the ring off. And P.S., you didn't do anything wrong. The sensible part of my brain pipes up, and I stop to wonder if that's true. Did I take off my grandmother's ring—the one that had the power to hide me from any magical being with the added double whammy of shielding my mind—because I wasn't hiding? Or was it more because I couldn't stand the reminder of why I'd needed it in the first place?

And am I really not hiding? I don't go back to my house. I practically sent Striker away. I can't bear to touch Ian...

Ian. Shit. I stood him up. With shaking fingers, I pull my cell phone from my back pocket, the simple act of it sending a hysterical giggle up my throat. His voicemail picks up, and despite my aversion to public speaking in general, I leave a message.

"I'm so sorry I stood you up. I didn't mean to." I pause, not quite knowing how to explain. "I promise to make it up to you. Call me back." I hang up, while I check my surroundings. Just to be sure I won't catch a human off guard, I turn off the cracked sidewalk and duck in between the warehouse that conceals Aether and a burned-out remnant of a building that I faintly recognize isn't really a building at all, but the thought is there and gone in a moment. Snapping my fingers, I let my magic transport me back to the alley entrance of my shop.

I learned not so long ago that transporting oneself from one place to another isn't just for wraiths, other Ethereals can do it, too. But typically, witches can only accomplish it if they have a full coven—all working on the spell together.

I can do it easily by myself. It made me wonder what else I can do that other witches can't and vice versa.

I inspect the warding lines—or lack thereof—of my building, knowing I'd strengthened the wards as I left. Was it Ian who broke them all? It doesn't seem to be a thing he'd do—torching all of my wards—but I don't really know what Ian would do...

Not really. I'd always been too selfish to really see him the way I should. I probably still am.

I sniff the air, catching the scent of the ozone of spent magic that could be from the wards coming down. Or it could be from something else altogether. I don't like it one bit, but if someone tripped my wards, I need to know who it is and what they want.

Oh, and I need to make sure the super-duper magical ring is still in my jewelry box, and the bone blade is still in my safe. Yeah, that wouldn't hurt either.

My nerves are shot, but I sack up—or I would if I had

a sack—and reach to turn the knob of the reinforced steel door I'd installed after the whole Micah mess. I'd needed the security, or at least the illusion of it. I probably still did—the little security blanket wouldn't hold off the ghosts, but would let me pretend they wouldn't touch me, anyway.

The hallway opens up to the back staircase, stairs I'd already trudged once tonight, but I bypass them to head to my office. Flicking on the desk lamp, I peruse the room. There isn't a paper out of place on my desk, no drawers knocked akimbo, nothing. But I have every certainty there was someone here. Maybe not now, right at this second, but my wards came down on purpose, and someone was in my office.

My safe hasn't been tampered with, nothing has been touched, but someone has been here all the same. I spin the dial combination, the same one that could blow the arms off a deity if they so much as looked at it wrong. Using every bit of magic I had, I'd made that safe so it was coded to only two people on this planet. Only two people could touch it.

Striker and me.

Anyone else would be blown to kingdom come and rightly so.

The locking pins disengage, and I swing the door wide, the bone knife—the same one I'd used to kill

Micah—sits on the velvet-lined shelf, not even a millimeter out of place. The low light catches the slight sheen of the ancient leather-wrapped hilt, the blade itself the length of my forearm, and the pristine color of freshly carved bone.

I know for a fact the blade is as ancient as it feels, carved from the humerus bone of an Ethereal a millennium or two ago. My mother never said what kind, but if I had a bet, I'd go with either angel or demon. Either way, I probably don't want to know. All I know is that blade makes me very uneasy, and the way it meets out death is sadistic and cruel. It makes me hate it and everything it stands for—everything it is.

It makes me ache in places just thinking about it, all the hidden places in my soul that I so rarely shine a light on. Great bleeding places that hold all the hurt and hate and pain. I hate how it was me who got free from Micah and Melody didn't. How I failed her so spectacularly. Hate how her son will never know her, never know what his mother went through so he could live. I hate how the brightest light in Striker's life is dead and gone, lost in a way she can never be found.

My skin begins to itch, and I shudder, the pain and heartbreak washing over me, threatening to drown me if I let it. I'd never failed someone like I'd failed Melody.

Never messed up so bad that someone died who didn't deserve it.

I've never had collateral damage before. Not in four hundred years. I find I'm not too keen on it.

I shut the safe, leaving the blade right where it had stayed for the last few months. I'd been unwilling to touch it. Hell, I still didn't want to. Spinning the lock, I study the safe, looking at the hex lines of magic that still seem as strong today as they were yesterday. I inspect them, making sure there are no breaks, no open spots, and just for kicks, I send another jolt of my power into the ward, strengthening it just a bit more.

I have power to spare lately, power I don't want or need, but what I accidentally drained from Micah. It's wrong, accidental black magic, but like so many things about myself, I can't change it.

I can only hope that one day I'll be able to get rid of it.

The trek upstairs seems longer the second time as I whisper the warding words of protection on my temporary-ish home. After ensuring the giant aquamarine ring my grandmother gave me for protection is right where I left it, I slip it on my finger before bedding down for the night.

Can't be too careful.

A tap on my shoulder the next evening causes me to nearly maim one of my best clients. My customer, Jet, is a man of few words and seriously opposed to small talk. We also differ greatly on what we call music, so as is custom, the pair of us have in our own earbuds—him with his preference of death metal, and me with a mix of just about anything else. I've been alive for quite a while, so my taste runs along the eclectic, but that is a genre of music I just can't seem to get into.

My new receptionist, Della, takes a few steps back, either frightened at the expression on my face or just jumping because I found my feet in a not-so-nice way, brandishing a dirty tattoo machine.

Not cool.

I set down the machine so the needles won't stab anyone, flick off my gloves, and pop the earbud out, looking Della over for a split second. Medium-brown hair pulled into a wispy yet complicated chignon, small build, fair skin so very different from my darker golden bronze. She's cute in a mesh of class and the everyday-girl way that I will never be. I will always be different, other. The blue hair and tattoos just make me feel more at home in my skin.

Virgin-skinned and proper with a Frenchie-Catalan

accent that drives my male customers absolutely wild, I hired Della on the spot after searching for a receptionist for weeks. She'd whipped my appointments into shape and had me booked out into the next year using some sort of administrative sorcery I'd never be able to cobble together. And she makes the best damn coffee I've ever had. She is a quiet little mouse of gloriousness, and I don't want to upset that balance.

But I feel like a first-rate idiot, especially since Della's green eyes are wide in fear.

Whoops.

"Sorry. You startled me," I murmur apologetically, taking a deep breath to calm down. It's completely possible that the PTSD-suffering person—me—should not be wearing earbuds in public. Noted.

"So sorry! *No va ser la meva intencio espantar-te.* You have a phone call." She's flustered, pointing behind her to the phone. My first language was Catalan, but Della speaks the more modernized version of the one my mother spoke to me four hundred years ago, and it isn't one I regularly use. Just like English, every language changes over time. I think she said, "It was not my intention to scare you," which is nice enough and makes me feel like a dick.

"Sure. I'll be right there."

She nods and backs away, and I tap Jet on his meaty

shoulder to let him know I'll be right back. He gives me a shrug, which could mean anything from "sure" to "whatever" to "I hate you."

Jet doesn't say much.

I get to the fancy new phone Della requested so she could do her job properly and pick it up, waiting for her to press the button for whichever line my call is on. I didn't hold the super expensive phone request against her. Before we only had a vintage rotary phone that would probably be at home in an old-timey whorehouse. Given the number of calls we get for appointments on a daily basis, her request for an upgrade wasn't too outrageous.

She presses the third blinking light—how she remembers which one is which is a freaking miracle to me—and the voice of my best friend comes through the line. I'm not even sure he's really my best friend at all—not sure if he has ever really trusted me the way I did him once upon a time. Not sure if it hasn't just been a convenience for him to hang out with me all these years. I hope not, but hope is pretty much all I have at this point.

His voice is husky as if he's just getting up, and I'm so happy to hear from him that it takes a few words for me to wonder if the huskiness isn't from disuse, but from screaming.

"Max! Max, Jesus, I'm so glad you're all right. You have to ge—"

His words are cut off as the power goes out. No more than a second passes from the lights spluttering out to my front picture window blowing in, glass flying everywhere right before the flames engulf the walls, the floor.

I soon realize what Striker's words should have been. They should have been "get out."

4

MAX

I never should have come back here. That is my very first thought as I stare at the flames licking their way closer to me. The bite of glass against my palm only serves to prove that thought true.

The words "collateral damage" flash like a neon sign in my brain, proving to me once again that maybe I'm not as good a person as I thought I was. Would a good person bring trouble to those around them? Would a good person stick around when they knew death was on their heels? Would a good person taunt their betters into firebombing their shop?

Probably not.

I sit here frozen, figuring I probably deserve the heat of the flames, deserve to burn. But it's the whimper of fear behind me that snaps me out of my self-deprecating thoughts. Reminding me it isn't just me in this room or this building.

In this fire.

I whip my head to the side and take in Della. She's crouching behind the mirror-fronted receptionist desk, the glass cracked in some places, shattered in others. But Della isn't the only person in this shop. I have two other artists here today, plus their customers and mine, Jet. Bellows of fear meet my ears for the first time since the fire started, but they seem far off, distant somehow.

A buzzing whine overtakes the yelling, the tinny, warbling sound making me wince, my fingers reaching for my ears before I can stop them. My hands come away red, blood thick at my fingertips. It's then I feel the slight tickle of a drip coming from my nose.

Was there a blast and I missed it? Or is this a spell? The world goes dark for a second, but I manage to shake my head enough to clear it a little.

The way out the front is completely blocked, the fire spreading up and out like fingers searching for light in the dark. I whisper a blessing of protection for Della and me and snatch up her hand, hauling her up with me as I search for a way out amongst the now-smoke-filled shop. I used to think I'd know my way around this place blindfolded, but the acrid smoke filling my lungs tells a different tale.

Crouching low, I manage to slam my shoulder into a doorjamb of the hallway before seeing the outline of the back door. "Do you see the door?" My voice is a guttural rasp, but she doesn't answer me.

I shake her hand, probably squeezing her fingers too hard. "Y-yes." Her voice seems a whisper when it probably really isn't. Everything is a whisper. Everything is a muted form of gray when I know it is really vibrant oranges and reds.

This is a spell. I look down, sluggishly searching my hand for the ring that was supposed to bring protection. Naturally, it's missing.

I glance back into the now-black void of my shop. "Go. Call for help." I need to go back. I need that ring and the bone knife, and I need to save those people—the innocents who were so foolish to find themselves close to me.

"No. You need to come with me." Her hands now becoming the firm ones, pulling, dragging me to the door. The air hits my face, fresh and clean and the pair of us huddle, gulping in the glorious oxygen.

"Here. You dropped this. Keep it close." Her words are coming in between gasps, my grandmother's ring in her palm as she offers it to me. "The working in the smoke is meant to confuse, I think."

I nod my head for a second, plucking the warm metal

from her hand until her words register, and I focus on her face. Della's human—or she's supposed to be. How in the hell does she know about workings?

Who the hell is she?

I don't have the time or energy to figure out exactly what species Della is, or what the fuck she's doing in my shop. She's helping me, and at the moment, that is really all I can ask for. Sliding the ring on my middle finger, my mind becomes clear again, like a fog lifting. Before Della can move, I have her throat in my hand.

"Who are you?" My hand is gentle but insistent. I want an answer before I give her my back to get my people out.

"Not your enemy. Your grandmother sent me to look after you. I'm an ally." Her voice is calm and soft but firm in a way I know her mouse routine was just that—a routine, a mask. Or maybe not. Eyes wide with fear, she unsuccessfully tries to hide her trembling. The faint scent of fear is in the air, and it's coming from Della.

"Good," I mutter, dropping my hand. "I'm going back in there. You helping?"

She shifts her feet, eyes sliding to the door and back to me. With a twist to her lips, she nods.

The door is warm to the touch as I throw it open. The heat and flames not yet reaching the hallway, but the sickly smoke wafting from the fire feels like fetid oil on my skin. Rancid, spoiled, sour. The air is ripe with it, the smoke like rotten fingers poking, prodding. Trying to get in my mouth, my nose, my lungs. The working is strong, meant to confuse, intended to reach into one's mind and make them sit there while they burn to death. It feels like old, forgotten magics. Not Celtic, not Santeria, not anything I've ever seen, but familiar all the same.

I hold the breath in my lungs, praying Della's doing the same. Without knowing the origins of the spell, I can't stop it, but I might be able to hold it back enough to get my people out.

Blowing the last of my breath on my fingers, I mutter every Latin word I can think of for "Stop" as I spin the working breath on the tips of them, the spell strengthening with every widdershins—or counterclockwise—revolution. Undoing, unraveling. *Subsisto, tardo, confuto, concesso, subflamino, insisto, conquiesco, finis*... Over and over, driving the fetid smoke back inch by inch, the green of my magic shines like a beacon in the dark.

All too slowly, the smoke recedes. Problem is, the fire itself isn't magical, so smoke or not, my shop is still a big ball of flame. I can't push the smoke back and douse the flames at the same time. The faint wail of sirens sound in the distance, but they feel too far away. We could all burn before I could even get anyone out of here.

Della moves around me, stepping close in the scant space between us and the spelled smoke weaving her way to the booths. Everything seems to move in slow motion. The smoke, Della, my nulling spell.

The smoke is too powerful. I feel it pushing back against me, searching for a break in my power, like a sentient thing. Intelligent in a way that means only one thing—the person who cast it didn't just throw the spell and leave.

They're still here. Pushing against me. Searching for a weakness, a break. Any fissure in my powers that they can weasel their way into.

I don't have the luxury of time. Whoever is casting this is stronger than me.

"Get them out." I choke. "I can't hold this much longer." The sweat at my brow isn't just from the heat of the flames. This working is kicking my ass in a way that I've felt before. This isn't witch work. This is a freaking demon.

I'd bet on it.

Della comes from behind a hand-painted silk screen, a man thrown over her shoulder in a fireman's carry. From the tattooed back of his head, I know it's Jet, and Jet isn't small. Confused customers and both my artists trail like a line of ducks behind her, heading toward the back.

I don't know if I should be confused or relieved. I'm sticking with relieved. Whatever super-strength mojo Della has, it's helping me out in a huge way. My only hope is Jet and the rest of my people are okay.

The sirens get louder, but the spell doesn't abate. The caster doesn't care that humans are in here, doesn't care that they could have killed someone. They want something, and they really don't care who they hurt to get it.

I can think of only one thing in my possession someone would kill to have. Something people have probably killed several times over to have, throughout time, and space, and worlds.

A shiver works its way through me.

All of a sudden, I feel cold. The spell I'd been pushing against falters, and I almost sag at the reprieve. But it doesn't last.

The sirens, once so close they were screaming, fizzle out as if someone turned the sound off on the world. The roar of the fire, the way it ate through my shop, the crackle and fizzle and pop of flames all silent.

My body trembles and I scramble back, half-searching and half-escaping to the office.

Whoever they are, I know what they want, and I'll be damned if they get it. Not from me.

I spin the dial on the safe, my shaking hands missing the last number and I have to start all over again.

Shitshitshit.

The locking pins make a shuddering snap when they release, but before I open the safe door, I yank the silver chain from my neck. Wrapping it twice around my right wrist, I pull the blade from the protection of the safe and loop the last bit of chain around my hand and the knife, pricking my finger on the tip and smearing the blood along the hilt.

Whispering ancient words of a magic I barely understand, the silver liquefies, the links transforming into a rope of metal, binding the knife to my hand. The hot metal burning my skin in a way that I know I'll scar, maybe in every healed body that comes back.

I try to think of the vanity of it instead of the pain. Instead of the smell of burning flesh. Instead of how this binding might be permanent. Instead of the blood and death magics I just used to protect the very thing I hate.

I whirl, watching as the flames freeze in place—unmoving, unwavering. The smoke itself like gray fog clouds hanging in the air. My shuddering whispers are the only sound, my lips the only movement.

Until I see the shape of a man, his form made up

solely of black smoke, flickering and wavering as if he has no corporeal form. Only his eyes are solid, unflinching, glowing yellow and piercing through the dim. They follow the length of my arm, tracing down my body until they latch onto the blade practically soldered to my hand.

The blackness rushes me, and I scramble back, scrabbling in a truncated crab walk until my back hits the plaster of a wall. And still he comes, a screeching scream of rage and wordless command vibrating through the ruins of my shop.

I slash with the blade the way Aidan taught me to, aiming for where the soft spots would be on a human. I know full well it won't kill whoever it is who seeks it, but a knife is a knife, and any weapon is better than nothing.

Aidan taught me that, too.

The screech of command morphs into one of pain or rage, the form backing away, retreating at my paltry slash.

And somehow someone turned the sound back on in the world. The sirens scream, men yell on the street. The roar of flames return.

I snap my fingers on my left hand, the action smarting a bit with a cut finger, but that's the least of my problems.

Traveling from my burned-out wreck of a shop, I arrive at a door in the middle of a dim hallway. *Numera omnes qui ingrediuntur ad iudicium.*

Judgment comes to all who enter.

Before I destroy the carved mahogany of the high courtroom door, all I can think is, *you're fucking right it does.*

5

MAX

The wood splinters, exploding into the too-perfect high courtroom, making my lips tip up just slightly. The ghost of a smile flits across my face and it's gone in an instant. Rage wars with the betrayal in my gut. How could they do this to me?

I know I told them I wouldn't kill Andras, but burning out my shop? Putting all my people in danger just to steal a freaking weapon? If they wanted the bone knife, they should have just fucking asked for it.

Barrett's surprise as he recovers from his cowering crouch in front of the dais warms my cold dead heart. Shards of wood pepper the floor, and his expensive loafers slip on them, making him unsteady on his feet. If I were to guess who on the Council ordered the firebombing of my shop, Barrett would be at the top of the list. Hell, Barrett would be the entirety of the list.

"I want to know why," I croak, the soot and smoke still clogging my throat even though this air is fresh as a damn daisy. It pisses me off. I want to rub my soot-covered self all over the pristine whiteness. I want to smear it with my blood. I want to spill it, too. Maybe Barrett's, but maybe not.

The dark side of myself, the one that I try to keep buried, wants to know if Barrett has friends or family. It wants to put them in danger instead so he knows how it feels. It wants the equal and opposite reaction, wants true vengeance. True reparations.

Fury like I've never felt courses through me. It should feel warm, right? It should be a fire under my skin, but it isn't. It's cold, icy. A frozen tundra of rage ready to exact my will.

"Why what? Fates, child, what in the name of perdition happened to you?" He appears almost... concerned? The fake worry on his face makes me want to slap him right across his snooty freaking mug. Maybe with my right hand—the one with a knife attached to it.

"For a man so keen on the rules, you sure know how to break them. I want to know *why* you firebombed my shop. *Humans* were in my shop. *Humans*, Barrett." I watch the ambient white of the room take on a green cast, my magics rising in and out of me so much I tint the room in their glow. The heat of them feel like soothing flames, masking the agony of the blade in my hand, the smoke left over in my lungs.

"I didn't—" He scrambles back a step, slipping on the wood again.

"Then you made someone or bribed someone. You want this blade so bad, you come and get it."

As I speak, the path from me to him cracks and shakes, the floor vibrating with my powers as it continues to rise in me. I've always hated a bully.

The marble floor shifts, peaking at the crack, the movement tossing Barrett off his feet. He scuttles back, trying to get away from me, muttering something under his breath. Not Latin, not French, something I've heard before but can't place.

Other than a zing of heat flashing over me, his spell does nothing. No blood, no broken bones, no flames, just a big load of fuck all.

My power rages again, shaking the foundations of whatever this place is. It feels neither here nor there, not on Earth, but not in Hell. Not Heaven. It feels like nowhere and everywhere, and me and my rage, my power is breaking it apart. The sick part of me smiles, happy at the destruction. It's hard to hold back on this newfound bloodlust, this call for vengeance and death. The siren call of retribution.

"Stop, Maxima. I didn't hurt your people. I didn't."

Then the distance between us is gone, the fingers of my left hand around his throat, pinning him to the cracked dais. "You wanted me dead from the moment I walked in here. Told me as much. Why should I believe you now?"

"Because I believe in the law, and hurting humans is above all the worst thing I can do."

The truth of his words take a minute to filter through the bloodlust, through the call in my brain that tells me to rip into his flesh with the bone blade and watch as his innards paint this stupid white floor red.

Truth. His words smell of truth.

My magics flare again, and I wish I could say they were healing me, but they aren't quite doing the job anymore. My stomach pitches suddenly, nausea and pain bleeding back into me bit by bit as my adrenaline wanes.

Barrett looks afraid, and I don't know if that fear is guilt or something else. All I know is I feel tired.

Tired of it all. Tired of fighting and getting nowhere. Tired of people dying. Tired of never being accepted, never really having a family. My rage peters out, and all I'm left with is...

"You sneaky little shit." I level Barrett with what is

probably my best glare. "A tired spell mixed with what? A depression or self-loathing one? Fates, you're diabolical. I didn't even see your lips move."

A wry grin peeks out of the cloud of his face, and he straightens fully away from my hand that has fallen from his throat, and that's when I notice Marcus sitting in his seat at the dais, his feet crossed at the ankles on top of the table, a bag of chips in his hands. He munches on one as he surveys us, the crunch of it practically echoing through the room.

"She could have killed us both, and you're eating bloody *crisps*?" Barrett dusts off his suit jacket and straightens his tie. His cultured British fading away to a less-polished version that he seems to hide.

"I told you she was going to kick your ass one day. Didn't think it was going to come so soon. I didn't want to miss it," Marcus says around the food in his mouth.

"No help at all. Sitting there eating bloody crisps. She could have *killed* me."

"And if you sent someone to hurt her humans, you would have deserved it. I was doing my Council duty to act as witness to either your sanctioned death or her crime. You're a twelve-hundred-year-old witch against an untrained Rogue a third your age. I assumed you could handle it."

"You're a right tosser is what you are. Against a

witch and demon hybrid that shouldn't even exist! It's like a house cat going after a Bengal tiger. One of them is an apex predator and the other *is not*."

His words are like a blow, a sucker punch when I was already going down. *Shouldn't even exist.* I feel my face go slack, the laugh at their exchange falling off my lips. Marcus catches my expression before I can wipe it clean.

"That isn't what he meant, Maxima. Barrett wouldn't be Barrett if he didn't accidentally insult someone every five minutes. You'd think he would be a better conversationalist by now, but he kinda sucks at it." Marcus' tone is consoling, and if Barrett's words didn't echo what I already thought about myself, it probably wouldn't sting so bad.

I give Marcus a tremulous smile, the spell Barrett cast still pinging every horrible thought I've ever had about myself through my brain, making his words fail to ring true.

"If you don't mind, please call me Max. The only person who calls me Maxima is my mother, and she doesn't like me much."

Barrett whips his head back to me, the anger sliding off his face as he winces. "Oh, *damn and blast*. That wasn't what I meant at all. And after that spell… bollocks. Maxim— er… Max, I didn't mean *shouldn't*." He sighs, covering his face with a hand in exasperation.

"But existences like yours are rare. As in you're the only one I've ever heard of. Demons and witches can't reproduce. The babies die. Every time. You just being alive is an anomaly."

"Just what every girl wants to be called, Barrett. An anomaly," Marcus grouses, uncrossing his feet and setting them back down on the floor.

"Fates, save me. That is not what I meant."

"You going to hoard all the chips? I think I'm going to need some if we're going to watch Barrett try and pry the foot from his mouth." I hold my hand out to Marcus for a chip but smile at Barrett so he knows I hold no ill will.

Plus, if Barrett didn't send that... thing to set my shop on fire, he isn't my enemy. I don't need to make him one. I have a feeling I have enough of those just being me without adding to it.

My eyes fall to my feet, and I finally grasp the full scope of my destruction. Broken marble, shards of wood, and rubble litter the floor. Like an angry child, I broke this room, shattered everything in my path.

I know it might just be from Barrett's spell, but the urge to cry hits me. One of the only things I learned from my mother all those years ago was that once you cast a spell, you have to be prepared for the fallout. There is no reversing anything—not really. All spells have to run their course. I can fix something once it's broken. I can give someone a memory back. I can even heal a papercut if I really concentrate.

But spells like the one Barrett hit me with will always run their course. Knowing that makes the sting in my eyes fade just a little.

Breathing a spell on my fingers, I snap them, watching as the green fire of my magics flare. Then the rubble moves, going back where it came from like an explosion in reverse. Every mote of dust, pebble of marble, and shard of wood go back to their original homes. The peak in the floor where the marble fractured flattens, the crack in the stone sealing before my eyes. The mahogany shards and splinters piece together before sealing back into the door as it once was. As if I was never here. I turn back to them, and Marcus stares at the door slack-jawed while Barrett looks at the floor as if it's about to jump up and bite him.

"What?"

"You do realize a whole coven of witches your age couldn't do that? Not to this place and not to that door." Barrett doesn't take his eyes off the floor as he talks, and I'm almost glad. But that last bit of magic seems to have spent all that I had left. My rubbery legs carry me up to the bottom step of the dais, and I plop down hard on my ass.

"We've already established that I'm a freak, Barrett. No need to rub it in. And while we're at it, can someone get this thing off?" I whimper the question while waving my charred ruin of a hand that still clutches the bone blade. I've tried not to look at it, but now that I have, I don't feel so good.

The blood starting to drip from my nose doesn't help matters, either. The bright white of the room begins to dim and then cants a little to the side.

Then it's lights out.

6

IAN

24 HOURS EARLIER...

My hands shake a little as I smooth the close-cropped hair on my head before doing the same to the goatee on my chin. It is a nervous tick my brother points out every opportunity he gets —usually when we're playing poker, and I'm losing.

I lose a lot. Kinda like I'm losing now, but only at a much different game.

I'd lied those many months ago—by omission, sure—but lying all the same. I never told her I knew her, knew the way her lips tasted, knew how her body fit to mine. Knew her scent when she was aroused.

I know lots of things about Max that she never told me.

At the time, she'd been nothing but an insanely beautiful girl sitting alone at a booth where she definitely didn't belong. In the midst of the chaos around us, she wasn't trying to sex-up a random stranger or make a deal when no one was looking, which was usually what places like that were for. All she did was people-watch and sip her drink. But the closer I got to her, the more I realized she wasn't a girl. Despite her young, unlined skin, this woman was old—older than me and probably wiser than me, too. Her eyes were the dichotomy of young and ancient, having seen too much and yet not enough.

I found myself sitting at her table without a real thought in my head, only that I wanted this beautiful woman with the intricately tattooed skin and blazingly blue hair to smile. I can't rightly remember what I said to her, only that I flirted and charmed and crowded her in the way wraiths do when they see a mate. Testing, teasing for a reaction.

And I got it.

But I never got her name, and a few weeks later when we came to Kyle and Nicola's rescue, Max was there. Broken and bleeding, she didn't remember me. And it hurt to think I didn't leave the same impression on her that she did me.

In the light of day, we hated each other. Well, that

wasn't true. I hated that she didn't remember me, and she hated that I was an antagonistic asshole.

Until about eight months ago when she died in my arms.

The fear and agony of that day echo through me as I stare at the back door of Max's shop. She lives here now, instead of the craftsman over on Lincoln, and a part of me hates that for her but loves how close she is to me all at the same time.

But all that could change tonight. Her closeness might be an agony instead of a balm. Because I have to tell her about that night in Aether. I have to tell her, and I really, really don't want to.

It takes another five minutes before I sack up enough to get out of the car, the threat of losing her creating a vicious noxious hole in my chest where my heart used to be. The trek to the back entry is long, each step weighing me down, but eventually, I get the door open and traverse the stairs even though my feet feel like lead.

At about the third step from the top, a hint that something is wrong trickles into my brain. There is no music. No movement. Nothing. I can't rightly say how she lived her life before, but every time I have ever come to visit her, Max always has a TV on or music playing. Always. As if the silence physically grated on her, she methodically made sure there was something going on in the background.

And there is nothing.

The second? I can't feel her magic anywhere. Max has an aura, a presence that physically presses in and lets you know she's there. It's comforting when she's happy and almost grating when she's angry. It's the light caress of her magic even when she isn't using any. It just is.

I've only felt it gone once, and any time she isn't where she said she would be, I lose it a little. I should have noticed before now that I couldn't feel her. I should have noticed before I ever walked through the door, but I was so worried about how she'd react to our history, I wasn't paying attention. Now my senses are on high alert.

Pulling in the scents from the hallway, I get a faint hint of someone who shouldn't be here. Ruby's signature fragrance filters through my brain, but it's nearly gone now as if she left in a hurry. Max's, however, lingers, her scent clinging to almost every part of this building. But there is something else, too. Something made of smoke and death and... something I can't place.

I take a few more steps up the stairs, my feet light this time, instead of my idiotic plodding when I wasn't paying attention. I strain to hear something in the building—breathing, walking, anything.

Something's wrong. Someone's here, I'd bet my life on it, and it's not Max. Calling on the power I assume I got from my mother, I cloak myself in the darkness around me. Sometimes I think this is the dumbest ability I could have gotten. I'm half-wraith, and I can't travel. I'm half-witch—*I think*—and I can't do half of what witches my age can. The only thing I can do that they can't is make myself essentially invisible. When compared to traveling, healing, and soul-eating, it's a neat party trick but has few practical uses.

This just so happens to be one of them.

But pain lances through my head before I can take another step, ripping a groan from my lips. I manage to duck the heat of the next blow, but my cloak of darkness falls from me as soon as I can no longer concentrate on it. Blood trickles down the back of my neck as I haul myself up the last few steps. Like an idiot, I don't have a weapon on me. How long has it been since I've gone anywhere unarmed? And yet—when it comes to Max—I never seem to think straight.

Despite my best efforts—and the lucky instance of my wraith eyesight—I can't actually see my attacker. The scent of magic rising fills my nostrils, cloying smoke-filled power like a perfumed house on fire. My whole body freezes, caught in a web of control, agony lighting up my senses so much it steals my breath. Whispers—low, commanding murmurs bombard my brain, but I can't quite make out what they're saying.

Odds are, I don't want to know anyway.

My eyes frantically comb the stairwell, searching for a hint—something, anything to tell me who or what's here.

My power flickers, sputtering once, twice before I'm able to cloak myself again, wriggling from the invisible binds of magic to Max's door. Turning the knob, I fail to feel the zing of magic that usually accompanies just knocking on it.

It's unwarded. Unprotected.

Max hasn't had an unwarded anything since Micah Goode attacked her. Not that her wards did much to keep him back in the first place, but that doesn't stop her from checking and rechecking them. Making sure they're as strong as she can make them.

But before I have a chance to let the worry fully consume me, the agony hits me again, and all I see is blackness.

MAX

Barrett's face is the last thing I want to see when I open my eyes, but that doesn't stop the man from being three inches from my face when I finally regain consciousness. Granted, Barrett is pretty if you don't mind the giant stick up his ass. Shockingly clear-blue eyes set in a pleasingly attractive face, square jaw, not too overly bushy eyebrows, decent medium-brown hair. Problem is, his face is perpetually dialed to disapproval.

Even now. I just woke up from a major magical cat nap—okay... I passed out from using too much magic and probably shock—but still. No relief. No "thank the Fates you're not dead."

Nope.

Barrett and my mother probably get along like freaking gangbusters based on their general level of disapproval alone.

"Don't look so disappointed, Barry. I'm sure I'll die at some point, and you'll get the joy of watching me come back to life. It'll be a hoot." I groan, planting a hand in the soft plushness of a pale linen couch to sit up.

It's then I notice I'm no longer in the white high courtroom, but what appears to be a stately office, and not Caim's, either, even though the courtroom and his office are both somehow located in Aether.

And yet not.

Then I start giggling, and Barrett's eyebrows begin their ascent up his forehead.

"I just got it." I'm still chuckling. "Aether. Everywhere and nowhere. The road to all places. No wonder there are so many pockets here. Speaking of, where the hell am I? I mean really. Is this Aether or somewhere else?"

"Somewhere else," Barrett murmurs, sitting down on the edge of the carved mahogany coffee table. "And you're right. Aether is like a hub. It connects places, makes the world smaller, and all that. Not everyone can travel like you, so we needed a thin place where we could move easily."

I find it more than a little disconcerting that he knows I can travel, but I decide to stay on task.

"A thin place?"

He rolls his eyes up, scanning the ceiling as if it holds all the answers. My guess is it doesn't because he heaves out a sigh before answering me in a cautious tone as if he doesn't want to say too much. "Places where the barrier between this world and the next is thin, where it's easy to traverse along the ley lines to get where we need to go."

"You mean the Veil? Because the Veil is a person— three people, actually."

His eyes fall back to me, the blue in them blazing.

"Yes and no. The Veil keeps the dead on the plane they're supposed to be on. They are the barrier that keeps our worlds separate. But demons don't need to use the Veil to go to Hell, just like angels don't need it to go to Heaven. We aren't bound by it because we're alive, hence thin places."

His expression turns speculative and assessing, and I don't like it one bit. I obviously know more than he expected me to, and rather than wallow in just how uncomfortable that makes me, I decide to go for moxie.

"You're telling me I could open one of the doors in Aether and walk right into Hell? Please remind me never to come back here, mmm-kay?"

"I'll make a note of it."

The door behind Barrett opens, and Marcus strides through, a black old-timey doctor's satchel in his hand. "How's our patient?"

"Alive. And inquisitive. You got the things I asked for?"

"Yes, I got your frankenbag," Marcus grouses, passing over the satchel. "You sure I didn't need to bring chicken blood and a sacrificed goat, too?"

"Nah, not this time," he mutters in all seriousness—either in sarcasm or just not realizing Marcus' joke, and I can't decide which one is more frightening.

"All right, Max, I need to get that blade off your hand, which means I need to perform a *break*. Have you done one of those before?" Barrett asks as he starts pulling items from the bag. A small silver bowl no bigger than my hands cupped together, a squat black candle with runes etched into the wax, a large vial of salt, and a few bunches of dried herbs tied together with twine.

"Kinda," I hedge. I mean, I have performed a *break*, but it didn't exactly go well—for me. The last time I did one, I had a demon compelling me to do his bidding, and I ended up burned at the stake, so you know...

Not exactly a point in the win column.

"It's a simple spell, but the blowback can be anywhere from infinitesimal to life-threatening. It is better if the person who cast the spell in the first place performs the *break*. It minimizes the blowback."

That doesn't sound good at all. More like it seems like an excellent way to fuck this up royally.

Here goes nothing.

7

MAX

I should have gone back inside the wards, but I didn't. Instead, I followed the sounds of agony to find a man clawing away from the warding snare. It didn't matter that he flashed back and forth between what I assumed was his true form of semi-solid black smoke and his glamour of a human man—the snare still caught him.

Something about the man called to me. I'd never seen an Ethereal like him. Our coven was secluded—hidden away from everyone and everything else who moved in the shadows of our world. He felt familiar in a way that I could not deny.

I had to help him. Had to.

But the only way to help him was to drop the wards—to put my family in danger. It was wrong. It was the worst idea I could think of.

"S-s-s-s-save m-m-m-me..." The thought hissed through my

head, but I knew I hadn't heard a sound. It wasn't my voice, it was his.

"I will," I promised, but I didn't tell my mouth to do so. It was as if my mind had been taken over by someone else. The closer I got to him, the more I needed to do whatever I could to make sure he lived.

Without my mind telling my feet to do so, I pivoted toward the hex marks of our covens' ward, snapping the protection spells one by one until the snare around the man's foot fell away.

"S-s-s-s-save m-m-m-me…"

Then I found myself whispering words I didn't know—spells too advanced for my young body to handle. In my head, I screamed to stop, but I couldn't halt the Latin falling from my lips or the charged green light flickering from my hands.

I was not in control, and I had a sinking feeling that this man, whoever he was, had taken over my body and my powers to free himself. Blood dripped from my nose, and I crumpled to the wet bracken of the forest floor.

I had to get away from him—whoever he was—before he took control over me again. But I didn't get the chance. The sound of hoofbeats hit my ears, and their simple squelching echo was enough to put a pit of fear in my belly.

Horses meant men. Men meant humans. Humans who could have seen me do magic. Humans who all too frequently burned women alive for even the assumption of practicing magic.

I didn't have enough time to put the wards back up. I didn't even have enough time or energy to run.

A pair of footmen grabbed me by my elbows, wrenching me from the forest floor and away from the man who was anything but.

They shouted at me, calling me witch and demon. They spat in my face and tore at my clothes, searching for a devil's mark. It wouldn't have mattered if I didn't have one. They thought I killed the man who was lying so still in the mud and leaves he appeared dead. They saw the green light coming from my hands —they saw my magic.

They tied me to a tree, took a lantern from the coach and threw it at my feet—the glass and fuel exploding as it hit.

Flames caught the cotton of my dress first, and sooner than I thought possible, I was left to scream out my dying breaths alone as men watched me burn.

"Max. *Maxima.* Max!" Barrett's voice filters through the haze of the last time I performed a *break*. But I'd never done one on my own—never of my own free will. Never without that man or demon, or whatever the hell he was speaking for me.

Ruining me. Destroying everything I was and everything I would be. My sight finally focuses on

Barrett, and I debate on whether or not I should tell him the truth.

"I—I haven't performed a *break* in a long time. The last time..." I trail off, almost unable to say it, the tremor of my past fear and agony rippling through me. "I was burned at the stake, and even then, it wasn't me who did the spell. More like it was done through me. So I'm more than a little rusty."

Barrett takes a moment to digest what I just told him.

"This was why you were named Rogue, isn't it?" Barrett whispers. "A demon compelled you to perform a *break*, and you got caught by humans. You burned for a crime you had no intention of committing." His voice is like ice, his blue eyes burning like the coldest of flames.

"I woke up in a charred circle. My mother threw me some clothes, told me I was Rogue, and I've been on my own ever since. Later, I figured someone thought I was a necromancer or something. Because I came back. But my mother never taught me any kind of spells, so me summoning a demon didn't seem to be on the table. Until a month ago I didn't even know I was half-demon."

The room seems to go cold—which honestly, I don't mind because my hand feels like it's on fire, but then it's Barrett who's looking at me, so, defensive positions may be necessary. Marcus also doesn't seem to be faring any better in the anger department.

"Ummm... guys?"

Marcus' voice is garbled, like his teeth don't quite fit into his mouth when he growls: "Your mother is on my shit list, Princess. I really hope I don't meet her in a dark alley anytime soon. I might have to get my mate to teach her some manners." His palm gently lands on Barrett's shoulder and squeezes, his touch appearing comforting rather than painful.

It takes me a solid minute to realize he means Barrett when he says "mate," and even longer before I realize he means that they both are pissed on my behalf. I'd always known Teresa had done the wrong thing—banishing me, blaming me for something I didn't mean to do—but I didn't realize how validated I'd feel. My nose starts stinging, and I have to blink away the hot tears that are just begging to fall.

"You know, your bickering makes so much more sense now," I crack, trying to bring levity to the room. Barrett's lips tip up, but it doesn't mask the outright sorrow on his face. It isn't pity, more like an empathy I didn't believe him capable of.

His voice is gentle, a murmur. "I'll walk you through the *break*. Step by step. It's simple. I've seen you do much more complex magic, so I know you'll be fine.

Quite honestly, it wouldn't be safe for me to do it for you, or I would."

"Now, don't go getting soft on me."

"Wouldn't dream of it."

Barrett walked me through the steps of the *break*, going over the proper pronunciation of the Latin. He didn't have to tell me that performing a *break*, especially this close to an object that was probably darker than the pits of Hell, was a little sketchasaurus rex—even for me.

I examine the Celtic runes carved into the black candle. There are three: one for protection, one for breaking obstacles, and one for water. Why there is a water rune on a candle, I'm not sure, but if we're washing away a spell, it sort of makes sense. I've always found runes odd in a way. Forgetting their names, but always remembering their definitions.

"Quit stalling." Barrett raises a chiding, knowing eyebrow. It reminds me of one of my mother's patented disapproving stares. I manage to slip off my grandmother's ring from the tattered ruin of my right hand and switch it to my left before I start, afraid the *break* will kill all the spells on that hand. Hell, I'm afraid of what the *break* will do to the blade itself.

I begin by drawing the circle with salt, whispering a blessing of protection before placing the bowl in the center. Dried angelica, rosemary, and sage go in the bowl before I snap my fingers to light it on fire, using the flame of the cleansing herbs to light the *break* candle. I blow the herbs out, letting them smoke enough so I can wash myself in the breath of the protection they offer. Only then do I start the chant of Latin, only part of my brain wondering why it is always a dead language used for spells and not English or French or Spanish.

Conteram hoc opus. Hoc carmen subsisto. Break this working. Cease this spell.

The more I say the words, the hotter the chain circling my wrist and forearm become, the metal burning my flesh until I smell it cooking. I try to shove the pain down but there is so much of it, it grows, builds, overflows my senses. I grip the bone blade tighter, needing to hold onto something, anything. But still, I continue my words, halting but true.

Conteram hoc opus. Hoc carmen subsisto.

The metal begins to melt, dripping onto the coffee table in a plink, plonk, splash. It's everything I can do to not start screaming.

Conteram hoc opus. Hoc carmen subsisto.

The metal is gone, freeing me from the blade, but I can't seem to stop chanting or let go of the dagger. The spell is in me now, working through me, taking control. Blood runs from my nose in a steady drip, drip, drip, and I still can't stop chanting the *break*.

Conteram hoc opus. Hoc carmen subsisto.

Oily black smoke begins to pour from the blade, hundreds of screams echoing off the walls as the room fills with it, dimming every light until the only source is from the flickering candle. Women's screams, children's, men's—all of them writhing together in a sea of pain.

Then everything stops. The pain, the screams, my chanting. Barrett seems to freeze in his half-sit, half-crouch on the ottoman to my right. Marcus, too, is frozen, only his is mid-shift. Gray fur sprouts from his arms and face, the bones of both misshapen with his change. The bone blade falls from my hand in slow motion, tipping end over end until it lands hilt-down before falling flat in the center of the salt ring, knocking the bowl of still-smoking herbs to the side.

My break didn't just free my hand. It freed something or maybe hundreds of somethings from the blade. The smoke begins to move, churning through the room until it finds an outlet—the fireplace. There, it funnels from the room until there isn't even a hint of the oily blackness. Only when it is completely gone does the candle finally flicker out, the room seeming to come back to life.

The light from the modern lamp at the side table flickers back on. Barrett finishes his jump to his feet. Marcus' phase completes, twisting his bones until a giant gray wolf is now standing where he originally stood. I look down at what was once a burned ruin of a hand. The flesh is knitted back together, only a red raised scar where the metal of the necklace once was.

"What in the fresh hell was that?" a terse voice calls from the door. The voice belonging to my very pissed off grandmother.

"I get a call from Della losing her mind about your shop being damn near burned to the ground, search for your impudent little arse for ages, only getting a blip on you before it disappears, and I get here—in Barrett and Marcus's house, no less—and you're doing arcane magic? Explain. Now."

I'm at a loss as to which part of her rant I should address first when Barrett, of all people, comes to my defense.

"Someone came after the blade, and she protected it, Bernadette. But she hurt herself. I instructed her to perform a *break*, and in doing so... Honestly, I don't know if we did a very good thing or a bad one. The *break* freed souls from that blade. Tortured ones."

Bernadette's face goes white at his words, and she half-sits, half-falls into the closest chair.

"Then it was a good thing," she whispers, her voice clogged with either fear or sorrow. It makes me wonder how many lives have been taken with that blade.

Makes me wonder if it stole their souls along with their lives.

Makes me wonder who made the blade in the first place.

Bernadette raises a shaking hand to her forehead, her voice husky as she speaks. "I came to warn you, my girl. You need to check on the people you love the most. Because if you think bombing your shop is the worst he can do, you haven't been paying attention."

My body goes cold, which is a fucking feat in and of itself since I still feel like I've been thrust in an oven set to broil.

"The worst *who* could do?"

"Who else, child? Your father."

8

MAX

My first thought is Ian. The one I couldn't get on the phone. The one I was supposed to have plans with last night. I give my body a full pat down searching for the annoyingly slim device that means I can contact anyone at any time. I sometimes forget to be amazed on a daily basis with just how far we've come since the 1600s.

Yanking it from my back pocket, I'm freaking astounded to find the phone is not only charged, but it still fucking works. All the magic that's been thrown around just in the last five minutes alone, you'd think the EMP the workings give off would fry the fucker.

Thankfully not.

I try him again only to be shuttled directly to voicemail. His phone is off, or destroyed, or...

I can't even begin to try to contemplate that one. Instead, I do the next best thing and call his brother who picks up after only two rings.

"Joe's pizza shack. You got the cheddar, we got the dough."

There are times when I want to punch Aidan Keenan right in the face. This is one of them.

"Have you talked to your brother today?"

"No. Why?" Aiden's worry is practically palpable down the line.

"My shop was firebombed. I haven't talked to him in twenty-four hours, and we were supposed to meet last night. I got roped into some bullshit with the Council, so I didn't show." I glance toward Barrett and give him my best "you know it's true" eyebrow. "I tried calling him and his phone is shuttling me right to voicemail. Either he's so pissed he's blocked me, or something happened."

"First, the Council? What the fuck did you do? And second, have you even attempted a locator spell?" By my pregnant pause, he gathers the answer. "And you call yourself a witch. Isn't that Woo-Woo 101? Finding people?"

"I don't have anything of his."

Aidan scoffs, sounding like he's rolling his eyes

better than any man over three hundred has a right to. *"You're* his, dumbass. If you haven't figured that out yet, you're dumber than I thought you were, and after our last session, that's saying something."

Yep, punching him right in the face the next time I see him.

"Considering I haven't even kissed your brother, I'd say the possession bit is a little premature, but I'll try." I say it trying to act blasé about the fact that Ian is fucking missing, but my tone must venture too far into bored for Aidan's liking.

"You'll do better than try, Maxima. You find my brother, or else." *Or else* from a wraith guardian means a sight bit more than from just about anyone else. It means he would book me on a one-way ticket straight to Hell if I didn't find Ian. He'd suck out my soul and eat it.

Literally.

"I'll find him," I whisper and then hang up, carefully placing my phone on the coffee table before I smash it.

Ian. I should have looked for him last night. I should have called Aidan sooner. Why didn't I call Aidan yesterday?

"You happen to have a pendulum in that frankenbag of yours? I need to find someone."

But when the pendulum finally falls, I find I don't want to be within a mile of where I know Ian is.

Looking at it from the street, the house seems no different from others on the block. The white, two-story craftsman shouldn't seem foreboding, but it does. I haven't been within fifty feet of my house—a place I used to think of as my sanctuary—in over a month. A cold chill races up my back as I stare at the cerulean front door I'd painstakingly repainted last June, which is a feat in and of itself since it's blisteringly hot for an August night. Denver cools down considerably in the evening, but not enough to cause the gooseflesh racing up and down my arms.

No.

That is caused by the blind panic that has me poised to run from what used to be my home instead of going inside to rescue Ian from whatever brought him here. There is no way he'd come here on his own. He knows how I feel about the place—as if the ghost of Micah Goode might be waiting in one of the darkened corners to come and snatch me up. But the grass is cut, the flowerbeds weeded, as if someone has been keeping the place up for me. As if I'm on vacation or something instead of afraid of a silly pile of bricks.

I don't want to be here. Not on this street, not on

this sidewalk, not anywhere close to here. But Ian is inside, and if I follow my gut—which I'm prone to do, even though it has brought me nothing but trouble—Ian is in danger or hurt, or a prisoner, and I don't have the luxury of the time a panic attack will take.

A bird's hair-raising shriek has me looking over my shoulder to scan the dark street. The call is close, and my eyes drift up to the lamppost where a falcon sits. In Colorado, it isn't uncommon for falcons to roam, but I've never seen one in the city, and sure as hell not on my street.

Another shiver races up my spine, focusing my mind on the task at hand. I assess my property lines, knowing the warding that keeps people away is long gone. I wonder what someone looking out their window at this hour thinks of my getup. Before my shop was firebombed, I was in my usual work attire of a tight tank, sailor-style pedal pushers, and heels. Now, my hair has fallen from the painstakingly styled victory rolls, my clothes are covered in soot, and somewhere along the way my shoes came off, so I had to conjure myself some flats. Plus, the black leather belt with the dagger sheath containing the bone blade doesn't exactly go with this outfit.

I've never been so thankful for nightfall.

Keeping my eyes peeled, I make my way to the front door, hesitating only a moment or twelve before I manage to turn the unlocked knob. Convenient, and creepy as fuck, because while I don't have my keys, it isn't like I coded the front door with my fingerprints. Someone wants me to be able to enter, and that just feels icky on a bevy of levels.

Then the door swings open and sitting in the middle of my living room is Ian, bound to one of my dining room chairs. He's unconscious, battered and bloody, his once-white-T-shirt spattered with the rusty brown of dried blood. It feels as if my heart has shriveled up and died in my chest, and I find myself rushing to him, sliding on my knees on the hardwood just so I don't knock him over.

"Ian. Ian, can you hear me?" I pat his face until I realize that I quit patting three pats or so ago and now I'm outright slapping him to get him to wake up.

"Ian!" I shake him in between untying the ropes that bind him to the chair. But he doesn't respond, and the only hope I have is the fact that he's breathing, albeit shallowly.

My brain goes into damage-control mode where it offers anywhere from easy to ridiculous ways to solve a problem, and the best I can come up with is to call Aidan.

"Where is he, Max?" Aidan barks down the line as I try to hold Ian's unconscious body upright in the chair.

"He-he's at my house." I shiver, the pain and shock and sheer weight of the day crashing down on me. "I-I can't get him to you. He's been knocked out, beaten. His breathing is shallow, and I don't... I don't know what to do. Help m—" I don't get the word out before the call disconnects and Aidan appears in my living room.

Aidan looks livid—a wickedly sharp sword in his hand glints in the meager light as he scans the room. Without so much as a hello, he grips Ian's shoulder and seems to think about it for a moment before snatching up my wrist. Aidan does that wraith-style voodoo smoke-out thing and transports us to the brothers' living room. Vomit rises in my throat when we land, me on my hands and knees, and I try not to chuff on Ian's carpet.

"I swear to the Fates, Maxima, if you don't get your shit together, so help me..." Aidan trails off through ground teeth as he lifts his brother onto the pool table.

I know that pool table intimately.

I damn near died on it.

Melody *did* die on it.

Staggering to my feet, I shuffle over to the table as Aidan cuts open Ian's bloodstained shirt with trauma shears and starts checking him over.

"What happened to you?"

Resting a hip against the solidness of the table, I ignore his question. "Is he going to be okay? Do I need to do anything?"

"You just stand there and tell me what the fuck happened to you. Had I known you'd look like you'd been drug through a tree backward, I would have had a bit more sympathy." He pulls a stethoscope from Ian's black doctor duffle, pressing it to different spots on Ian's ribs.

"My problems are less important than your brother's life, so just focus on him and don't worry about me."

Aidan pops the earpiece out of his ear, leveling me with a hard stare. "I have to worry about you, because for some reason, your shit keeps landing my brother in hot water. I have no doubt Ian was handed over to you like a present, giftwrapped and everything. So you'll tell me exactly what's going on."

Forgiving his delivery, the man has a point. Ian has been through one thing after another, and while it hasn't always been my fault, I certainly don't help matters. "The Council picked me up last night for the murder of Micah Goode. Sentenced me to death and everything until I reminded them I was an unwilling participant in Micah's schemes. Then they asked me to kill my father. I said no, and then today my shop was firebombed by a black smoke demon thing who tried to kill me."

I don't even want to tell him about the blade and the souls I accidentally released. Or the fact that I blew up the Council's front freaking door. Yeah... Aidan is pissed enough.

"I swear to the Fates, I rue the fucking day he met you in that stupid farce of a club. 'Go to a witch club,' he said. 'We'll meet hot chicks,' he said," Aiden grumbles as he check's Ian's pupils. "Well, he makes out with a woman who doesn't even remember him, and I damn near get my ass blasted off in that raid. Seriously. Ian should have listened to Caim and left you alone, but *noooooooooo*."

Ian made out with a woman in a witch club and then there was a raid. A woman who didn't remember him. The puzzle pieces all click together.

"You're telling me it was Ian this whole time? And no one thought to tell me? I ought to punch you right in your stupid face, Aidan Keenan."

The look of surprise on Aidan's face would be pure gold if I didn't want to murder him so bad.

"Is he going to be okay?" I nod toward Ian, sparing him the briefest of glances so my heart doesn't decide to wrench right out of my chest.

All this time.

I've been so hung up on that guy. The one that woke me up, made me feel. And he was right in front of me the whole time. I feel like an idiot.

"A concussion, maybe a bruised lung. He should be okay."

"Good," I murmur, my voice as soft as I can make it before I throw my fist right in Aidan's stupid face.

9

MAX

The line rings less than once before one of my best friends on this planet picks up.

"I really hate it when you wear that stupid ring, Max," she says by way of greeting.

Never one to mince words, that one. Aurelia hates it when she can't see me, and by see, I mean *see*. As a phoenix seer, Aurelia is a weird sort of psychic. If she's close to you, she can tell where you are, what you're doing, and, sometimes, what you're about to do.

If she's not close to you—and I mean emotionally—then she can only tell when and how you're going to die. More the how than the when. But all that death makes my BFF a might bit odd. If PTSD and emotional family drama had a baby, that baby would be Aurelia Constantine.

"Well, not wearing it seems kind of stupid right about now." I examine the ring that I've moved back to my right hand, the skin still red and raised where the metal burned through my flesh. It will, without a doubt, scar, and I wonder if I die and come back if those scars will stay with my body.

"That doesn't sound good. Why don't you tell me what happened?" She says it in the form of a semi-demand. Yep, that's my mother hen of a best friend. It doesn't matter that I'm twice her age, Aurelia would boss me around even if I were a hundred times her age.

"My shop got firebombed, Ian got attacked, and the Council is up my ass. Did you even know we had a Council? I can only assume whoever did it—and fun fact, the person who did it is more than likely my absentee father—wants to make an example out of the people I love, so... This is my friendly check-in to make sure you and yours are alive and well."

Silence permeates the line long enough to make me wonder if the call dropped, and I begin to pace the length of Ian's room, the only quiet place in this joint. Well, the living room is pretty quiet, too, but that comes with Aidan's bitchy stares, and I can't deal with that right now. I'm too amped up from everything; I can't deal with his pissy silence.

"Nope, we're all good. At least so far. I'll put Tweedle

Dee and Tweedle Dumbass on alert, but whoever wants to tangle with a houseful of Aegis is going to be in a world of hurt. Is Ian okay?"

I can only assume Tweedle Dee is her husband, and Tweedle Dumbass is the Wraith King—AKA Aidan's boss. That should be a fun conversation. I sometimes forget Aurelia can electrocute just about anything, and her twin sister Mena is probably the most powerful phoenix to rise from the American Legion in two thousand years. And that doesn't even take into account the fact that my tiny friend could take the head right off a man's shoulders with one precise strike.

"He will be." I rake a hand through my wet tresses, the cleanliness of my shower leaching away as reality sets in. My friends are in danger because of me and my fucked-up family.

"Then I want to unpack some of that shit. Your *dad*? I could have sworn Teresa hatched you like the bitchy reptile she is."

I was afraid she was going to ask that.

"Not something I want to get into too much depth about. He's like a former crown prince of demondom or something. I need to do some research, but the consensus is that the Council wants me to kill him and then take the demon seat. And by the way, I saw the seats, babe. Phoenixes and wraiths have them and they're empty, so maybe you should check into that when this whole thing blows over." I huff out a breath, amending, "*If* it blows over."

"Why do I get the feeling you're trying to distract me from the fact that you've got some big shit going down and you're not asking me for help. Just because I can't see you doesn't mean I've lost all sense, Max." Her exasperated "Mom" tone is barbed enough to grate on me.

"Well, do you or do you not have two little ones in your care? Do you or do you not have a husband that will no shit fillet me alive if I get one tiny scratch on his beautiful wife? You're benched from hero duty until your babies can fend for themselves. Hunker down and spread the word. I have a few more calls to make." I want to explain this gently, but I'm too hurt from Ian and Aidan's betrayal to be nice. I'm too sore from the cut of my father wanting to kill me. I'm an open festering wound and I just can't be nice about her safety right now.

"I'll do that, but you be safe, too. I love you, Maxima, and watching you die was the worst thing I've ever experienced. Don't make me do it again, got it?"

"Got it. Love you back," I murmur before disconnecting and plopping my ass on the edge of Ian's bed.

My eyes drift to the man under the covers. A part of me wants to crawl under them and snuggle next to him, and the other part wants to patiently wait for him to wake up so I can give him another concussion.

I feel like a joke, but I can't seem to make myself leave this apartment until I know he's okay. I need to see his eyes open, and then I can leave. Maybe Denver isn't the city for me anymore. My shop has already been busted up twice, and people I thought were friends aren't who I thought they were.

And Striker. His betrayal still stings, and I still don't know how deep it really goes. He knew the shop was going to be attacked. Was he with my father? Did he hear something? I have too many questions when it comes to Striker and not enough answers—especially for a man I'd lived and breathed and worked beside for a century.

And then Ian keeps the club shit under wraps. It's just one betrayal too many. The very last straw to break me. I thought I'd found a home here, but if the last four centuries have taught me anything, it's that no home is permanent.

Not for someone like me. Not for a Rogue. Not for someone who has never had a home or a real family. One would think I'd be hardened to it by now, but every time, it still hurts when I have to leave. I've probably stayed here too long, anyway. I just need to make sure Ian is okay first.

———

A soft finger tickles the shell of my ear, and I can't keep the smile off my face if I tried. I'm warm, snuggled in the softness of a down comforter, unwilling to open my eyes to assess exactly where I am. Who I am. I could be this girl for a few more minutes. I could be safe and warm and so, so loved. But then the hurt and betrayal and all the poison of the last few days seems to filter through the happy haze my brain so desperately wants to hold onto.

I pull away, out of the ball I seem to have curled up in at the foot of Ian's bed, my feet on the floor and ready to run before rough, callused fingers close around my wrist, pulling me back. I fight the urge to fall onto the bed, but his touch alone is banking the fire that has blazed for years. The fires of hurt that never seem to really die.

"Where are you going?" Ian's voice is husky as if these are the first words he's spoken all day, and maybe they might be. But it's a question I don't want to answer. I pull my wrist from his grip, no real feat since he isn't giving me much resistance.

"Away." The word is curt, but no less true. "You're awake and healing up. I don't need to stay any longer."

But true to form, Ian is up and out of bed and in front of me, barring my escape.

"Wait, wait, wait. You're just leaving? No, 'I'm glad you're alive. Sorry you got your ass kidnapped and beat to shit for me.' Just going. I'm real glad you actually give a shit, Maxima, or my feelings might be hurt right about now."

Rage ignites in my belly, and I have to clench my fingers so I don't claw his freaking eyes out. "Oh, we're gonna talk about who hurt who?" I abruptly stand, ready to face off with him if I need to.

Ian moves closer, in my space, in that tiny little bubble where he shouldn't be. "Yeah. I want to talk about who hurt who," he murmurs, somber. Watchful.

"I know about the club, Ian. *I know*." Pain leaks into every word. "Why didn't you tell me who you were?"

"I—"

"No, I don't really want to hear what bullshit reason you have for why you didn't tell me. It doesn't matter. Because if you actually gave a shit, you would have before now."

"But—"

Again, I cut him off. "Save it. You made me feel like

an idiot. How many people knew, and I didn't? Huh? How many?"

How many people saw me as the moron who made out with a guy in a club and didn't remember him? How many people were in on the joke?

"I was going to, but... When you saw me again, you didn't know me. I figured you didn't care as much as I did, so I didn't say anything. Then the Fates kept throwing us together, and the longer I went without telling you, the more it would hurt when I did, and..." He trails off as he turns away to plop into the striped bedside chair. "I didn't want to lose you. Even if I didn't really have you."

His answer thaws the wall of ice around my heart just a little, and all the rage and anger and fight bleeds out of me.

"I thought about that night so much, I figured I must have dreamed you. But your face was hidden in the dark, and you never gave me your name. I didn't know who you were. You should have told me."

I skirt around the chair, needing to get the hell out of here. Ian doesn't need me, and if he actually gave a shit, he might have told me sooner.

"You're still going to leave?" he murmurs before his fingers clasp around my wrist again, pulling me around and back to him, my chest pressed against his. I focus on his throat until I see it bob in a swallow. Somehow that one tiny nervous action pulls my eyes up to his. Then his lips are on mine, the softness of them contrasting so beautifully with the coarse hair on his face. His palms cup my cheeks, holding me still as the pair of us sink into the kiss, and it's just like I remember.

Fast. Frenzied.

Our hands drifting anywhere and everywhere we can touch. Pulling on clothes, trying to reach skin. He really is the man from the club those many months ago. He really is the one I couldn't believe I'd lost myself with—lost and found myself. Found the woman who had just opened her eyes to how wonderful this world could be.

And then in true Ian fashion, he ruins it.

"You about done with that running bullshit?" Superiority leaks into every word. It's all I can do not to punch him just like I did his brother. The floaty feeling of happiness evaporates in an instant.

"Running keeps the people I love safe. Running keeps me safe. Running keeps my dumpster fire of a father away from everyone I freaking care about, so how about we don't kick running out of bed just yet, mm-kay?" I pull from his arms, his warmth, ready to bolt.

"It won't help. And as much as I want you safe, running now just means more running." Ian squeezes my hips, trying to get me to see his side. But he doesn't know.

He can't know.

My laugh is bitter as it spills from my lips. "Running is all I know how to do."

10

MAX

Leaving the bedroom is the only course of action I can possibly fathom. But in the finding of my phone and the bone blade and trekking through the apartment in Ian's T-shirt and boxers, I realize that I have nowhere to go. My shop could be burned to the ground for all I know, my house is tainted with the specter of Micah Goode, and I have no one else. No one that I would thrust the burden of my presence upon, no one I would endanger by asking for help.

My footsteps falter in the living room just feet from the front door, Ian on my heels.

"Max! Don't leave," Ian pleads as Aidan sits back on the couch, undoubtedly to watch the show.

"I just figured out I have nowhere else to go," I tell

the door, letting my once-proud shoulders droop. "I can't go back to my house, my apartment burned to the ground along with my shop, and if I burden someone else, my father could hurt them, too."

The silence of the fire rockets its way through my brain. I would have just sat there. I would have just burned. How can I put the people I care about in danger like that?

That would make me the monster my mother always thought I was.

"What do you mean your father? What do you mean your apartment burned to the ground?"

Aidan's dark chuckle echoes through the silence. "You've been out of the loop, brother. A lot has happened since yesterday."

"Yeah, a lot has happened. You guys are just going to get hurt if you help. I *can't* ask you to help." Heaving a resigned sigh, I reach for the door.

"You said it yourself. You have nowhere else to go. So why not let us help? You too proud for help?"

I think of how Aidan blamed me for Ian's kidnapping. There is no way in hell he's going to let his little brother stay anywhere near me, and honestly? I don't blame him. The knob turns easily in my hand, as if locking it never even entered their minds. Or maybe it's my sign to keep going and never come back.

"Yes," I whisper, but I don't give Ian a chance to try and stop me this time. As soon as I clear the door and the warding lines I placed last month, I snap my fingers —heading to the last place I want to go.

I'm trying to stay here the least amount of time possible, so the frenzied stuffing of all my shit in a duffle bag is looking a bit more like a tornado than I'd care for. This room in particular gives me the creeps, and if it weren't for the fact that the last vestiges of my wardrobe are here, I wouldn't step foot in the place. Plus, trying to pick which shoes to leave behind is becoming more of a nightmare than originally anticipated.

I don't want to leave Denver. I don't want to upend this life I've built for myself. But then again, I didn't want to be burned at the stake, or cast out of my coven, or have a murdering demon as a dad.

I don't always get what I want.

I sigh as I glance between the pair of electric-blue peep toes in my left hand to the sensible black wedge booties in my right. Neither of them will fit in the bag, and only one pair is even remotely comfortable. I put them both back on the wooden rack in my closet, and whimper at the fashion sacrifices I'll have to make in the coming days.

I suppose when this all dies down, I could have Aurelia send me my things, but I have a tough time wagering free tattoos and warding spells for that big of an ask. I move to the final thing to pack—besides weapons—that I always bring with me to a new place. The last scrap of fabric from the dress my mother gave me after I was cast out. It seems stupid that I've carried it with me for so long, but I can't seem to let it go.

It's a reminder.

A beacon.

A way to remember to never get too comfortable. Never drop my guard. Never trust that everything will be all right. This scrap is the perfect reminder that even family will leave you in the dust.

I pull the plastic bag from the keepsake box I usually keep on the top shelf of my closet, careful to keep the nearly four-hundred-year-old fabric from creasing. This is all that's left of the dress, the cloth decaying over time. The first time a piece crumbled to dust I cried for a week. Now, there is so little left, I fear I won't have it for much longer. I gently stuff it in an internal pocket of my duffle and return to the closet to pick from my small cache of weapons.

Aurelia loves Christmas, and her favorite kind of gift

to give is bladed weapons. I can't blame her, each weapon gifted is as beautiful as it is functional. She even taught me how to use some of them. My personal favorite is the rope dart. Silver and gold braided through thick twine all attached to the ringed handle of a carved iron push-dagger. Better than just pretty, I spelled the blade ages ago with a working to keep a wound made by the blade from closing.

I also pick up a trio of throwing knives spelled with a *rue de sanguine* working that is lethal to most Ethereals. That is if I don't miss. I put them in the bag along with the bone blade, unwilling to carry it on my person.

Not after I freed those souls. I may never use it again.

The only other thing I need is in my casting room, a spiral-handled athame that has been with me since my first day of my new life. I nicked it from the refuse of where our encampment had once been before I was kicked out. Someone had left it behind. For a long time, it was the only tool I owned, and that blade, and my power and the scant amount of knowledge of witchcraft I had was all that kept me alive back then.

I turn the blade over in my hand, knowing the secrets it carries.

How many lives it's taken. How many lives it's saved.

Slipping the athame into a small sheath at the base of my spine, I gather up my duffle, not surprised in the least at how heavy it is. I glance around the casting room one more time before walking through the basement, up the stairs, through the kitchen, and out the back door. Passing my now-unkempt greenhouse, I snap my fingers, carrying myself to my shop.

I arrive on a rooftop across the street from the burned-out wreck of what used to be my tattoo shop. I haven't called my artists or the insurance company. I haven't dealt with the police or informed our customers that we were no longer in business and wouldn't be for some time. I didn't do any of those things in the scant time since the fire, even though it feels as if it happened ages ago.

The brick still stands, but every single window has been blown out, glass still littering the sidewalk below. The wide-arched antique panes of glass are now nothing but rubble. The brick stands tall, blackened with soot that still seems to smolder. I remember buying this old wreck of a building years ago. It took forever to restore it —make it new again.

And now it is nothing. The roof yawns wide with big gaping holes, the support beams sticking out like toothpicks into the night sky, blackened and charred. It feels as if a piece of me burned to ash right along with my building.

Too focused on what remains of my livelihood, I

don't notice the man behind me until he's a little too close for my liking. Closing in fast, I'm not sure how I can feel him, but just knowing that I can, sends a chill down my spine. But chill or no, it's not like he gives me a head's up before he strikes, all fangs and claws.

Sloppy.

Aidan taught me how to duck strikes the hard way, so this bumbling man is a bit easier to evade than, say, a wraith guardian. I duck him and quickly reassess that he might not be as unskilled as I originally thought. His flailing attack puts me right in the scope of another man I didn't sense. A man whose touch is pure ice—so cold it seems to burn through the thin fabric of my shirt.

I want to scream, but I can't. All I feel is coldness, all I sense, all I see, is the frigid ice of my own torture. Then a wicked specter of a chuckle floats to me on the high winds of the rooftop. It's a bitter, mocking sort of laugh I know well—even if the only place I hear it now is in my dreams.

The last time I heard it, I was in my house trying not to die.

Then the cold is gone, and my body wilts to the pebbled surface of the roof. It can't be. My nightmares can't be real. There is no way this can possibly be happening.

But it can, can't it? I performed a *break*, now, didn't I?

All those souls, hundreds, maybe thousands of souls trapped over the ages. Stuck in the putrid home of a bone dagger.

And I set them free.

I set *him* free.

Micah. Goode.

Had I known when I wielded it that the blade trapped souls, I'd like to think I wouldn't have used it. I'd like to think I couldn't be that cruel.

But I know what I've done in my past to men like him. I know what lives I've taken when there was no other way to survive. When it would save a life. When it would stop an evil.

I know—for Micah—I would always, will always pick up whatever weapon I could use to stop him. And maybe this is my comeuppance. My punishment for knowing such a horrible thing about myself and refusing to stand down.

But Micah isn't alive, I know that much. His body—such as it is—is only slightly opaque. The colors just on this side of gray, his flesh just on that side of sallow.

But he can touch me, hurt me, burn me.

And we both know it.

"Did you miss me, Maxima? I sure missed you."

The hope I held that I wouldn't hear his voice again

crumbles to dust. I thought the laugh would be the worst of it, but *noooooo*.

This motherfucker has to be able to speak too. Micah Goode is proof positive that no good deed goes unpunished.

"Nope, I didn't. I figured the knife in the chest would have been a big enough sign for you, Micah, but even from the fucking grave you want to torture me. What is it? My birthday? Are you the Hell gift that keeps on giving?" I try to keep him talking long enough to grab the small vial of salt stashed in my duffle.

But just like in life, he intercepts me, latching onto my hand as his clumsy friend wraps his cold arms around me and squeezes.

"I think I might like this better, Maxima. I'm not hungry, I'm not thirsty, but I have a need, and that is to make you pay."

In all the time I've walked this earth, I've never seen a spirit like this one. When souls aren't claimed, when they aren't sent on by a phoenix to be reborn or a wraith to writhe in the pits of Hell, it isn't like they just stay with their bodies chilling in their graves until someone gets to them.

Ghosts move, but they aren't aware. They don't interact with us—not really. Some might follow their family, their loved ones. Some wander, searching for that one thing, that last piece of unfinished business.

But Micah... he's aware. He knows who I am and how he died.

He is vengeful.

Spiteful.

And drawn to me.

The cold steals my breath, and in my desperation, I haltingly mutter the only spell I can think of. *Exillium. Banishment.*

Micah's spirit doesn't leave exactly, but the spell—as halting as it is—does push him back a few feet, his shoes solid enough to make twin trails in the graveled rooftop. The weaker specter, the one holding my arms, lets me go, and I fall.

And I don't waste the scant opportunity I've found. I rip the zipper open on my duffle, finding the vial of salt and the rope dagger. I manage to pour a handful of salt in my palm and run the braided metal and twine rope through the grains. Salt in the rope, iron in the blade. I may not be able to banish or even kill Micah Goode.

But I can hurt him.

From my knees, I toss the dart. And miss. The blade sails past Micah, hitting nothing but air. But my wide shot isn't without its virtues, because even though the dart misses, the rope finds Micah just fine.

His howl is uniquely satisfying, but my good fortune doesn't last. I pay too much attention to Micah and forget his bumbling friend. He spins me so I'm facing him now, and for the first time, I see why he might be so awkward.

Half his face is gone, his body burned and crippled in his mask of permanent death. He doesn't speak, only moans his happiness as he burns me again and again with his icy clutches.

"*Ex—exillium,*" I whisper through the bitter pain, praying the spell works even for a second.

But I don't get that second—not with two players in the game. The grotesque spirit lets me go, but Micah latches on, and even in death he got to keep his talons. And his fangs.

He strikes with both, cutting into my arms, his fangs piercing my neck, spilling my blood onto the rooftop, unable to drink it. He swallows again and again, but the blood falls through him, drip, drip, dripping.

Water, water everywhere and not a drop to drink.

I don't realize I've said the words aloud, until his hand scores icy fire across my cheek.

"Shut up! Shut your fucking mouth, you stupid bitch!" He drops me back down to the rooftop as he rakes his hands through his hair. Even as a ghost, Micah sure is vain. In his frantic pacing, I manage to slip my hand behind my back, latching onto the handle, drawing the athame.

"Aww, wassa matter, Mikey?" I slur, the pain and blood loss seeping into my bones. "Can't finish the job?"

He growls, ready to hit me again until I throw the athame. This time I actually hit my mark—even if it isn't his heart where I aimed. True aim or not, the athame remains lodged in Micah's belly, the silvery blood staining the blade when he draws it out.

"How many people have you killed that way? And now you can't get the job done. Must sting a bit, huh, Mikey?"

Micah drops the athame, moving to rush me, but he stops so fast the pebbles beneath his specter feet skid. His eyes go wide before his mouth twists into a rueful sneer, and just like that, Micah Goode runs for his life... or his undeath, if you want to get technical.

I want to look behind me, but as dumb as it sounds, I'm just too scared. I don't have much else in my grasp except for the rope dart, and honestly, I don't think it will do much for whatever it is Micah would rather run from than take his shot to kill me.

Heavy footsteps fall, slow at first and then faster, and still I can't make myself look. Squeezing my eyes tight, I brace for the killing blow.

A killing blow that never comes.

Warm hands fall on me where cold ones once were, and I know exactly who scared Micah Goode into running.

Opening my eyes, I prove myself right.

Ian came for me.

11

MAX

I want to ask Ian why Micah ran. Was it just because I had backup? Or was it something else? Something wholly Ian that made Micah run for the hills.

I know he'll be back. I know Micah isn't done with me. He has an eternity worth of time and nothing better to do. It might be time to ask Gramma how to banish a ghost.

Ian murmurs, *"Salutaris." Health, to heal.* It's a spell I've never been able to get to work on myself, but when Ian murmurs the faint Latin, I feel the blood start to clot on my neck. The working doesn't close the wounds entirely, but at least the bleeding stops.

"Fancy seeing you here, handsome," I slur slightly,

the healing spell doing nothing for my other wounds or the blood loss.

"You didn't think I was going to let you leave town and not say goodbye, did you?" He clucks his tongue. "You and I have unfinished business, kinda like those specters I seem to have run off. You picking up strays?"

He seems awfully calm for a man who's just seen a ghost. This isn't his first time seeing ones like that, and I don't know if I'm relieved he came to my rescue, or miffed I don't know this about him. I settle on relieved because, hey, I'm breathing, right?

"Not picking them up. They found me."

Ian's lips form a tight line but he doesn't say another word, his silence edging me out of grateful and into miffed.

"Care to share with the class why two ghosts ran for the hills just seeing you coming?"

His lips turn down in the universal sign of "nope" right before he grumbles, "Not particularly."

"Tough shit."

"I don't know why, okay?" His voice is like a whip as he throws up his hands. "I have a theory, but it's unproven and a shit one at that considering it's based on nothing but a guess. You're not the only one who doesn't know their parents, Max."

He has a point. I don't know the entire scope of what

I can do because the only demons I've seen have tried to kill me. It's not like I had the time to ask them exactly how my abilities work. And from what I gathered? Ian knows even less about his parentage than I do. His only benefit is he has a sibling he actually talks to.

"Let's get you up and back to the apartment. I can treat you there." He helps me stand on my unsteady legs, then his eyes fall on the athame still silvered with Micah's blood.

He inspects the blade, turning the corkscrew handle this way and that. "You managed to cut him?"

A flash of alarm has me standing on my own two feet and reaching for his hand.

"Don't get your face too close. If you turn that blade just the wrong way—"

The added feature of that particular blade springs free, a specially carved rune in the underside tang of the first turn of the corkscrew—a preloaded spell that lengthens the blade from dagger size to short-sword size. All of which that just manages to miss Ian's face. But he doesn't seem to be surprised so much as peeved.

"How about you don't mess with my weapons? I have a couple of secrets that don't need to come out in the form of your death, mm-kay?" I gently remove the athame from Ian's grip, pressing the rune again to shrink the blade.

He lets me go and reaches for my duffle, giving me a pointed look as he removes both the athame and rope dart from my hands. "I take it this was your doing? Altering the weapons?"

"Some, but the athame came like that."

"Interesting. Where did you get it?"

Why he's asking this while I'm beat to shit on top of a building after being attacked by fucking ghosts isn't just irritating, his tone is more accusatory than I'd like.

"Virginia. 1642. I picked it up from the refuse of a burned-out home. Left behind by my coven after they left me to rot. Any more veiled accusations you want to make?"

He only shakes his head, still eyeing the blade as if I stole it. As if it shouldn't be in my hands. I suppose I did technically take something that wasn't mine, but possession is nine-tenths of the law and all that. Whomever the athame belonged to, they didn't care enough about it to keep it, left it behind in the ashes of one of our coven homes, so it became mine. Bigger things have been claimed with less.

My cell phone buzzes in my back pocket. I swear the thing is indestructible at this point. The number is one I sort of recognize, a Coeur d'Alene area code, meaning it could be one of two people. My little sister or my mother.

I cross my fingers, answering, "Hello?"

"Ma—Max," Maria whispers, her voice aching and strained, making the tiny hairs along my arms stand on end.

"Ria? Baby girl, where are you? Are you hurt?"

Maria was ten when I was cast out. Neither of us really know our fathers. In my case, that's a good thing, but in Maria's not so much. At least hers was a good man, even if he left this world much too soon. One of my biggest regrets is leaving her to the iron rule of my mother, even as involuntary as my going might have been.

"Man… came… took Mom. Need help. Hurts…"

"*Ria!*" I want to smash something when the call disconnects. I'd rip a hole in the world for that girl, even if she isn't a little girl anymore. Even if Mom would rather pretend I never existed, and Maria just followed her lead.

Even if she never really loved me at all.

I wrench the duffle out of Ian's hand with probably more force than necessary, raking through the bag for a pendulum and an old road atlas from 1997. I use one of the throwing knives to pierce the flesh of the outside of my forearm, coating the edges of the blade in the fresh, untainted blood. This blood doesn't have spectral traces, wasn't drawn by ghostly fangs or claws. It's as clean as I can make it.

Smearing the blood on the pendulum, I pray this works. While we're only half-sisters, the bloodline is surely pure enough and close enough that the casting shouldn't be a problem. I spread out the paper map of Idaho on the pebbled rooftop, wishing that Google Maps worked with spells. Hell, the thing is magical enough on its own, how hard could it be to upgrade it a scosche for locating purposes? I mean, I can find the best Thai food in town, but locator spells are out of the question? Shenanigans.

"Max, what are you doing?"

"Shh! I'm busy."

Swinging the pendulum, I gather myself and my power, focusing on Maria's face, on my love for her. *"Ea invenio, invenire soror mea." Find her, find my sister.* The trouble with casting a locator is every single one is different. The spell is tailored for each person, each relationship, each circumstance. It depends on who you're looking for and on what plane of existence they're on.

So, when the pendulum stops swinging, the magic in the spell halting the rose-quartz crystal without dropping, without the pull to any one location, I fear the worst.

Tears track down my face, but I don't have the time or inclination to wipe them away. Maria asked for my help, she went to me when there are about a dozen other people she could have gone to.

She asked me, and I'll be damned if I let her down.

I try two or three more times before calm, warm hands find their way around me, softly pinning my arms down to my sides. At this moment, it doesn't matter if the hands are soft. They're stopping me, and Maria doesn't have the luxury of time.

"Max. Max! How about we try a bigger map? Maybe she isn't in Idaho." Ian whispers the last part in my ear, and it takes a second to register before I stop trying to claw my way out of his arms.

I nod, and his arms fall away, flipping the pages to a larger-scale map. If this one doesn't work…

I set the pendulum in motion again, murmuring the spell over and over. *"Ea invenio, invenire soror mea."*

The pendulum falls inside the confines of the state of Colorado, so I flip to the Colorado map and do it again. This time the crystal drops, the cut tip pointing to Denver.

I swear to the Fates, if this stupid thing points right back to me, I'll lose my damn mind.

Moving to the Denver city map, I swing it again, this time the pendulum is yanked out of my hands, the brass chain slipping from my fingers as the sharp crystal's point embeds in the map, landing in the warehouse district.

It's near Aether, and if I drive, I can be there in twenty minutes. Just snapping my fingers and traveling there isn't going to happen. Not after Micah. Not after however many times I did that stupid locator spell. My car should still be parked behind the burned-out wreck of what used to be my shop. Since my keys are more than likely still in what used to be my apartment, I might be able to use magic to start it.

Maybe.

I rip the crystal from the map, stuffing it back inside my bag. I'll need to get a new road atlas, but that's the least of my problems right about now. I need to figure out how to get off this roof. Preferably without dying.

No one has time for that.

Standing, I try to pull the duffel up with me before my weakness makes itself known. I sway, nearly going splat on the rooftop. *I guess it's better than going splat on the sidewalk.*

"Whoa, whoa, whoa. Where do you think *you're* going?" Ian tries to take the duffle handle from my grip.

I may be weaker than a day-old kitten, but he can fuck right off.

"I'm finding my sister."

"No, you aren't. You can barely stand up. Let alone help anyone else."

"I'm fine." Even *I* know it's a lie. My whole body feels like it has been simultaneously frozen and set on fire. My bones ache, my skin feels raw, and that's not even taking into account the scabbed wound on my neck.

I feel like smeared dog shit.

But my little sister needs me, and that supersedes everything else.

"Do I look blind to you?" he snarks, and I kinda want to swing this duffle hard enough to smack him in the face. I want to, but I won't. Because I'm a weak ass right now and I fucking can't.

"It's my sister, Ian. Would you leave your brother behind? Would you let him die alone and scared because you were a little hurt? No. You wouldn't. So, don't tell me I'm not going. I'm going. Either with you, or through you, but I'm going to find my sister." I seethe through gritted teeth.

"I'm not saying don't help her. Let me and Aidan go. We can find your sister."

He's talking reason, but I'm not having it. I don't know what mess my sister is in, and I'm not leaving her Fate at the hands of Ian and Aidan. At this point, Aidan would rather let me and my sister die just to protect his brother. I can understand the sentiment, but it doesn't instill much confidence in me being left behind.

"Aidan would rather throw me off this roof than let you go back out there and stick your neck out for me."

Can I blame him? No, no, I can't. Ian's face is still healing, the purple, almost black around the inside of his eyes, the swelling still there is faint. There are probably even more wounds I can't see under his black T-shirt and green hoodie. More than I can even dare to think about.

A concussion and probably a bruised lung. That's what Aidan said. Ian might be up and around, but he actually isn't much better off than I am.

"Let's call him, then," he taunts, tugging the bag fully out of my hands while he dials the phone. This time I don't try to get the bag back. It's too big of a feat to stay standing, the dizziness seeming to seep into every part of my brain.

Blood loss can just fuck right off.

Not a second later, Aidan arrives on the rooftop in a swath of black smoke.

"Weren't you leaving town?" He offers in greeting as he traipses to us, the confident swagger of a man with zero fucks to give.

Even if he's wearing a beanie on his head.

In August.

"My sister needs my help, but your brother won't let me go alone. Since standing is a bit of a problem, I can't exactly say no to the offer. You coming?"

Aidan's expression goes from taunting, to speculative, to concerned. Ahh, so he still does have a heart underneath it all. Good to know.

"Lead the way."

12

MAX

Touching down on the pavement, I barely avoid giving into my burning need to vomit. I hate traveling with Aidan, and the sadistic bastard only seems amused by my inherent motion sickness where this particular wraith ability is concerned.

Resting my hands on my knees, I take deep breaths to avoid all my internal organs hitting the sidewalk, and pray a little to any God, deity, or power that be that will keep me from chuffing on the pavement. Luckily, someone listens—either that, or my equilibrium finally settles from having all my molecules ripped apart and put back together wrong.

When I can breathe again, I take stock of the deserted street. There are two very different parts to Denver's warehouse district. The trendy, gentrified parts, and the deserted war-zone-looking parts. Every city has them, the places no one up to any sort of good wants to go. It makes so little sense why my family would be here, but since we're less than a full city block from Aether, the stretch isn't exactly thin.

I examine each building, looking for the tell-tale signs of warding sigils or hex lines. Something, anything that says a witch has been there. I'd take a neon sign spelling out the word "Trap" at this point. Walking west is my only option on this dead-end road, and I begin scanning each building for the luminescent pale-silver hex lines that only I seem to be able to see.

I'll never forget when Caim found out I could see and smell magics. I'd never felt so odd before, and that's saying something. Honestly, tattooing "freak" on my forehead would be a time saver for everyone.

Each building has the façade of a crumbling wreck, and no doubt some actually are, but others aren't what they seem—I know that much. I might not be able to completely see past their glamours, but I can see enough of the magic to know they are there. Granted, there is enough "go away" magic to fill the ocean, but those spells don't always work on me.

I blame the half-breed demon mojo for that.

But I'm looking for something specific: the silvery warding lines from a witch, which would surpass any glamour for security. But it's tough to see past the two men who seem to be trying to keep me from my end goal. Aidan and Ian both shadow my unsteady steps, one behind and one in front, in a dumb-as-shit protection sandwich that I want no part of.

I catch a bright spot out of the corner of my eye: flickering hex lines of a ward that is slowly dying.

"There." I point and take off running, drawing the energy from pure adrenaline alone. Or maybe from the scant amount of hope that still lingers in me.

I make it ten feet from the deserted husk of a building before Ian drags me back, his thick arm catching me by the middle. As someone who has never required permission from anyone, this new turn of events pisses me right off.

"That's a warding line. I see the hex marks." I try to explain before losing all patience and whisper-hiss, "Let me go, you idiot!"

Ian's arm goes slack, but he doesn't quite let me go.

"Do you have any idea how many Ethereals are in this part of town? Hundreds, maybe thousands. Just because you see warehouses and crumbling buildings, doesn't mean they are actually there," Aidan chimes in, and I'm so happy to have a wraith explain witch things to me.

For real. *It's my favorite.*

This takes mansplaining to a whole new level.

I resist rolling my eyes and punching him in the jaw again by sheer force of will alone. "I know. I can see past the glamours. I can also see the hex lines of a ward, and the sigils look familiar, so..." I trail off, staring pointedly at the arm still circling my middle.

Aidan gives Ian the man nod, a pretentious little chin tip, and I have to force myself not to light them both on fire. I maneuver closer to the building, careful not to step on a hidden ward or sigil, which is tough to do when there is trash and grime everywhere. Carefully, I approach the peeling wood of a door that looks like it's holding onto its hinges by a wing and a prayer, as I study the familiar hex lines keyed only to a specific bloodline, a hopeful smile curving my lips.

Teresa Alcado never could figure out how to keep me out.

Debating for half a second, I try to decide whether I should pluck the lines and let everyone in, or just walk right through the ward and leave the brothers behind. Tickled at the thought, I pick door number two, their curses following me in the building as I turn an ancient knob to the equally old door.

Inside, the furnishings are quite a bit nicer, that is to say, the ceilings are complete, and I can't see the sky. But while the walls and floor are new, freshly painted or papered, the room is a total wreck.

An antique red velvet settee is turned on its back, one leg hanging precariously by a thin splinter. One lone overhead light casts deep shadows on the broken remnants of the room, the smell of ozone from spent magic is high in the air. Walls are cracked, the plaster bowed or in rigid peaks as if it were exposed to a flash fire or an extreme heat. An upholstered chair lays on its side far from the circle of seating, its fabric slashed to ribbons. Smashed glass from broken lamps litter the thick pile on the Persian rug, their remnants lying broken, their cords wrapped around table legs like coiled whips.

But Maria isn't here.

Not in this room anyway, and I'm hesitant to carry on further if this is what the living room looks like. I can't sense another presence, and that is the part that scares me most of all.

Retracing my steps, I head back out of the ward and begin plucking the hex lines apart. I can feel the brothers' stare, but I don't explain—can't explain what's inside.

They have to see it for themselves.

"Are you out of your fucking mind?" Ian's hot whisper hits my ear along with the warmth of his breath. But it isn't just his breath I feel—no. His rage presses into me like a smothering blanket.

"Nope. Just tired of you two keeping me from doing my job. I thought I could go in there and get her but..." I trail off, shrugging as I pluck another hex line and watch as it fades away.

"But what?" Aidan asks from behind me.

"She isn't in the living room, and the place is blown to shit," I murmur, plucking four or five lines at a time, trying to get the ward down faster. "If she's in there, I can't feel her. If I can't feel her, then something else could be in there, too. Hence me unraveling these stupidly complex warding lines so we can all go in to be murdered."

Last one, I think and pluck the lone remaining hex line.

"Okay, it's down. Give me my weapons," I order Ian, who's holding my bag.

He unceremoniously drops it at my feet, and I crouch to dig through it, grabbing the throwing knives, bone knife, rope dart, and the athame. I don't know what's in there, and honestly, I hope I don't find out. But just in case I do, I want to be armed. I tuck the athame back in its spine sheath, stuff the throwing knives in my bootie, snap the clasp on the bone knife holster around my waist, and wrap the rope dart around my wrist, tucking my index and middle fingers in the loop of the push-dagger.

Aidan seems to be already through the door, and I move to follow him when Ian stops me.

"You be careful. Stay behind us, and no cowboy-martyr bullshit. I will knock you out to keep you safe, don't fucking try me."

More wraith bullshit.

Like my life matters when Maria is hurt or dying. Like my breath is more important than hers. I feel my magic rise in me, the crackling sort of power that flows from my chest, down my arms manifesting in green-hued molten fire skating over my fingertips.

"You get in between me and finding my little sister, so help me, I will put you down. I can't die. She can. Don't fuck with my family, Ian." My threat is palpable in the scant space between us.

Ian takes a step back, hurt tracing over his face before he masks it. I want to be sorry, but I'm not. I'm not sorry for needing to protect my sister. I'm not sorry for being willing to give my life —such as it is—for hers. Ian might not realize it now, but he'd do the same for Aidan. He'd steamroll anyone in his path to keep his brother alive.

Even me.

He heads into the building behind Aidan. The room

is just as decimated as before, only slightly more illuminated by the green tinge of my magics that I can't seem to suppress.

And I feel nothing.

Not my sister, not another presence.

Just... nothing.

That is until a tiny flare of something to my left pricks at my consciousness. Like a flickering flame, it sputters, ready to die out. I don't think, I run—past Ian and Aidan, and wrench open a battered door. Only with the added light of my magics do I now notice the faint smear of blood leading to the door as if someone was either dragged there, or maybe... if someone crawled there herself.

I don't see her at first, the closet too dark that even the feeble light from the room and my magic does nothing to penetrate it. Icy chills rake up my spine. This blackness is too big, too thick. Something is here, cloaking her, hiding her. My only hope is I have enough juice in me to knock the darkness back.

"*Detrahet me in lucem.*" I mutter a faint, breathy whisper of hope. *Bring me light.*

And then she's there, curled up in a bloody ball covered in heavy coats and furs. If it weren't for the blood, she'd look so much like the sleeping child I left behind all those years ago.

"She's here," I whisper-yell, alerting the boys so we can get the hell out of here.

I reach for her, ready to pull her from that abyss of a coat closet when a hard body knocks me away, slamming me into the floor. I try to breathe, but all the air is sucked away by a putrid, rotting-flesh-smelling... *thing*. I can't see what attacked me, but if I were to take a guess, a zombie wouldn't be far off.

Not that I think zombies are real, but if they were, this is exactly what they'd smell like. I reach for the rope dart, re-coiling it around my wrist, ready to let the dagger fly as I scan the room for what hit me. All I see is Ian and Aidan back to back, blades drawn and braced. Aidan is bleeding from a gash on his upper arm, and Ian is unsteady on his feet.

There are too many shadows in this room. Too many places for things to hide.

"*Detrahet me in lucem,*" I command, my magic rising in me and exploding from my fingers like the sun.

The spell bathes the room in light, the sources coming from all directions, all angles so that there are barely any shadows, and oh, how I wish I could unsee what resides in them. Crouched in a corner is a monster if I ever saw one. Naked, pasty flesh of a human body, the head of a crow missing its feathers, talons instead of fingers, hooves instead of feet. Ripped from the very depths of Hell, this is something that should have stayed in the dark. Its talons grip the sheetrock as if it is gearing up, preparing itself to launch.

And then it does, pushing off its great hooves, bypassing the brothers, talons reaching not for them.

But for me.

It's fast, darting toward me like a missile. The rope dart leaves my fingers before I ever tell it to fly, sailing around the monster's neck, the short blade of the push-dagger imbedding into the flesh there. Black blood as thick as tar pours from the wound, but all I've seemed to do is give it a leash for me, a tether to yank me from my feet.

And it does, it so does.

It reels me in until I have enough sense to let the rope go, but my hesitation means I'm down again, and all too quickly it's on me, taloned hands gripping my upper arms as it looks me over. Intelligent, ruthless eyes assess me and quickly find me lacking, the crow's head emitting a coughing sort of bird chuckle. It's mocking, derisive, and if the human shaped part of him had anatomy, I'd kick him right in the nuts.

Too bad he doesn't have any.

You think you can best me, child? I've been rending flesh from bone before humans even existed. There is no torture that I cannot create and no punishment out of my reach. You will not kill me, child. Not with your puny witch weapons.

"What do you want, then? A cookie?"

"Who the fuck are you talking to?" Ian whispers, and it takes a second to realize that they can't see what I can. They can't see this monster holding me hostage.

They cannot see me, silly girl. That's part of my charm. People fear more what they cannot see, cannot perceive, so much more than what they can.

I highly doubt if someone saw this monster they wouldn't fear him. Not unless they were stupid.

Tell them to leave. You can even have them save your baby sister. But you're staying here with me. We need to have a chat.

I nod, and the bird-human-horse man lets me go.

"Aidan, get your brother and grab my sister and get the fuck out of this house. Now." My voice is low and as calm as I can make it. Ian won't do what I need him to, but Aidan? I know he will—he won't even hesitate.

"What the hell are you talking about?" Ian hisses as his brother herds him to the closet.

Aidan reaches, pulling my sister's limp body from its depths, and I breathe a sigh of relief. Not because I'll be okay. I highly doubt I'll come out of this unscathed.

But because the people I care about will.

13

MAX

I don't bother looking behind me. I know what I'll see if I do. Ian's hurt, maybe enraged expression as his brother pulls him from the room. Maria's blood-covered face, her body barely clinging to life.

I don't need to look. I'm too busy standing in between the monster and my family. Too concerned with keeping his beak on this side of the room.

"I'm coming back, Max, and you better be alive when I do," Aidan calls from the door, his voice like an ice bath of vengeance and promise.

The last traces of my power crackles in my hands as I look over my shoulder, Aidan's coal-black wraith eyes taking over the green, bleeding into the white sclera, piercing me where I stand. I only say one word, but it's enough to shock even Aidan who probably cares the least about anyone except his brother.

"Don't."

I turn back to the crow demon, staring him down. Preparing myself in case he decides to go back on his offer of letting them go. If it came down to it, he would win. Probably. Aidan might have taught me a few new tricks in the last month or so, but training with him is a far sight different than fighting a demon in real life. Thankfully, this demon in particular doesn't seem to want to feast on my flesh.

At least not right now.

I feel it crackle in the air when they leave, my body bereft of them, even though I wanted them to go.

"Okay, they're gone. What do you want?" I cross my arms over my chest. It's a dumb stance, Aidan has told me so on a number of occasions, telling me to always be loose, ready. But I can't right now.

Relax, child, I am not your enemy. I take that back. I could be your enemy if you don't give me what I want.

No shit. That's the beak of a carrion bird if I ever saw one. Mr. Crow Man would eat me without a second thought and we both know it. "And that is?"

The blade, girl. Why else would I drag myself up to this frigid place? My master wants, I retrieve. It's not that complicated.

He's right. It isn't complicated at all. I don't even

consider it. Not after what I saw come out of the bone blade, not after what I felt. It is a soul stealer, and I won't let it fall into the wrong hands.

Not again.

"No."

Miraculously, the naked crow face morphs into what I assume is shock. I didn't think birds could have expressions, but hey, you learn something new every day.

What do you mean, no? This isn't a negotiation, girl. Give me the blade or I'll make you.

His talons reach for me, but I dance out of his way, the pair of us circling each other, searching for the right opening.

"What? You can't grab it yourself? It's right here." I point to the bone blade in the specialized holster Barrett gave me. Big Bird doesn't know it, but no one but me can remove the blade from its sheath, so I don't feel as worried about flashing it to my enemy. "Ahh, that's right. Demons need permission, even the lowly slave ones, isn't that so? Well, I'll make it as uncomplicated as I can. I'll never give up this blade. Never. Go back to your master and tell him I said so."

I don't think so, child. My master wants, I retrieve. I'll take you down to Hell with me if I have to, but he'll get that blade.

I don't doubt him, but even in death, I won't give him what he wants.

"Then we don't have anything else to talk about." I drop my crossed arms to my sides, adjusting my stance. My throwing knives are too far away in my boot, the bone knife is too precious to pull from its sheath.

But the athame, that can help.

I just manage to pull it when the demon is on me again, his talons digging into the flesh of my shoulders, his beak open and hissing right in my face. I didn't know crows could hiss, or maybe this amalgamation of species gives it abilities above and beyond that of the animals it portrays.

The speaking inside one's head thing is a major upgrade.

His beak lunges for my face, trying to pluck the eyes from my skull, or just eat me whole. His putrid breath speaks of the worst pits of Hell, of torture and rot. I swipe the blade, grazing him, but the pain is enough for him to let me go. My reprieve doesn't last long before he's on me again, ripping me off my feet and throwing me into the tatters of what used to be an opulent sitting room. *At least the Persian is soft,* I think as I suck in a breath, trying to find my feet. In the struggle, I dropped the athame, and I scramble to find it. My fingers close around the hilt and I slash blindly, forgetting everything

Aidan taught me, managing only by luck to catch him again with my blade.

It isn't enough. I'm not enough. My body is too spent, too tired from the toll of today to use any magic, and my strength—such as it is—is too weak to take on something like this.

His huge, hulking body knocks me off my feet, and I didn't even see him move that time. His talons pin my shoulders to the floor, before drawing me up off the rug. The sharp edges dig into my shoulders, cutting the flesh, but my hands are free, and I spin the handle in my fingers, pressing the rune as I bring the athame up between us.

The blade expands just like when Ian accidentally pressed it, driving up and through the soft spot on the crow's head, just before the hard beak erupts from his face. It drives deeper, through his head and out the top of his skull, pouring the black-tar blood all over us both.

His talons fall away, his body going slack as I wrench the blade from him, the tine sticking a bit in the bone until I yank it free. I guess *one* witch weapon was good enough to kill him. Pressing the rune again, the blade collapses and I wipe the black blood off on one of the ruined upholstered chairs and slip it back into the sheath.

Then I take a gander at the rest of me. Sticky black

blood covers my shirt, soaking it somehow, even though the blood doesn't even seem thin enough to do so. I yank off my outer layer, peeling the thin Henley from my skin. At least the tank underneath is black. I won't be winning a beauty contest, and I might be a touch cold, but it'll do.

I take stock of the room again, wondering what happened here, wondering what happened to Maria and Mom. Could this demon do this much damage? Probably. But it feels like more. It feels like I'm missing something big and I don't know what.

Keeping a watchful eye, I head back out the ancient door into the cool night, taking my first deep breath once the rancid smell of the demon is behind me. My bag is gone, but that isn't a huge surprise in this part of town. My only hope is one of the boys snagged it before they left, but I don't have much hope on that front. They had bigger problems than my stuff.

I pull my phone from my back pocket and start laughing. For as much as I thought the thing was indestructible, I guess it couldn't stand up to a fight with a demon. The screen is cracked, spiderwebs of broken glass and missing pieces. I'm amazed I didn't rip my hand open just pulling it from my pocket.

I guess this means I can't call an Uber.

That thought has me giggling. In the middle of the

night in a human-deserted part of town that likely has plenty of not-so-nice Ethereals teeming to fuck with the Rogue. There is a good fucking reason I never come to this part of town. I need to shut up, but still the giggles come, competing with the clicking of my booties on the pavement for loudness.

A man appears on the sidewalk not fifty feet in front of me, stealing my laughter. The dark swath of smoke curls around him and then dissipates, melding into the darkness around him. Hands in his pockets, he heads in my direction. I'd be scared in any other circumstance, but the beanie on his head gives him away.

"I told you not to come back for me," I nag, unable to say I'm glad he ignored me. Glad at least I have one person in my corner. Ian might not forgive me for what I had to do here tonight, and a part of me doesn't blame him. But I'm not sorry, either.

"Yeah, but I never listen to you, anyway, so why start now? Ready?" He doesn't let me nod before he takes us both off that street, the faint cry of a bird the last thing I hear before the darkness swallows me.

I hate traveling.

This time when I land, I don't have the strength to hold back, finding the closest receptacle to vomit in. Unfortunately for me, that receptacle is one of my lavender planters. Aidan, the kind soul he is, leaves me to my misery.

When my stomach finally gives up the ghost, I stagger through the back door of my house, not even a little afraid of the place. I guess that's fighting a crow demon from Hell for you, it will cure you of just about anything. My bag is sitting on the kitchen table, but otherwise the kitchen is empty. I follow the rustling sound of feet to my guest room where Ian is tying off the final stitch to a long gash in my sister's arm. There are stitches along her hairline as well, and if the mounds of bloody gauze and detritus of medical equipment are any indication, I owe Ian one.

Using the doorjamb to prop myself up, I ask, "How is she?"

"She'll be fine. Some deep lacerations, maybe a concussion. She'll be okay in a day or two."

"Thank you. For helping her," I whisper, grateful he was there, that he could help her when I couldn't.

He nods, not looking at me even though he's finished sewing her up, collecting the trash and bloody towels to avoid it.

"There was a demon in that room, Ian. You couldn't

see him, but he wanted you gone. Be pissed at me if you want to, but I did the best I could under the circumstances. Everyone's alive, so when you're stewing on it, please remember that."

He stuffs the rubbish forcefully into a trash bag pilfered from my kitchen, shoving the gauze unnecessarily hard into the plastic. Still not looking at me like a damn child. And in the grand scheme—at least compared to me—he is young. Maybe too young to understand why I would keep him out of harm's way.

Fed up, I sigh, skirting around him to reach Maria. Her skin is sallow with blood loss, but her breaths are even, and she appears peaceful in her sleep. I bend down, kissing her forehead, away from the stitches and leave her to rest.

When I look up again, Ian is staring at me, a mask of fury on his face. He sees my cuts, probably some bruises, too. The burns from Micah's too-cold touch, the blood both from me and the crow demon. He takes it all in, barring my way out like he'd love nothing other than putting me in a padded cell and throwing away the key. I feel a trickle of warmth at his concern.

But then it all comes crashing down.

"I can't do this anymore," he murmurs, not meeting my eyes. Instead he studies my injuries, cataloguing them, tallying them up in his brain. I can practically see it behind his eyes.

That trickle of warmth is long gone, replaced with a burning cold even Micah's touch couldn't surpass.

"Can't do what anymore?"

I want him to look me in the eye when he says it, when he tells me I'm not good enough. When he says that I'm too reckless, too crass, too different, too something. That I'm chaos and calamity, a disaster just over the horizon.

His brother has said as much, so why wouldn't he?

"I can't watch you throw yourself into one scrape after another with zero thought to who might miss you when you're gone. Aidan and I will help you with your father, but after that..."

He doesn't have to say it. I understand him just fine. *He won't help me anymore.*

"Don't worry, Ian. I know when I've worn out my welcome." I choke out, managing to hold back the worst of the pain.

Skirting around him, I'm barely holding onto the last bit of strength I have when I catch Aidan watching me from the hall. His face is an impenetrable mask, and I can't tell if he's happy his little brother gave me the boot or not.

It doesn't matter anyway.

I have a scrap of fabric in my duffle that tells me everything I need to know about people. A three-inch by three-inch square of wisdom stuffed in a Ziploc bag. Everyone leaves. One way or another.

I shoulder past Aidan, the shame and hurt and everything else hitting me all at once. And four centuries old or not, I still feel like a kid when I catch the trickle of tears starting their descent down my face. My mask breaking even though I thought I'd hardened myself enough over the years. I guess not.

I make it to my room, locking the door and heading to the shower. I crawl in fully clothed, only stopping to remove my weapons and boots. The water is ice when it hits me, but I don't really feel it.

All I know is no one can hear me break over the rush of the water.

And that's all I wanted anyway.

14

MAX

I sit crusty-eyed and cranky, curled up in the bedside chair next to my sister. If I weren't leaving town, I would set this chair on fire on my front freaking lawn. Hell, since I *am* leaving town I still might. I don't have any groceries here, so the coffee situation is dire. The whiskey situation, however, was just fine last night, hence the cranky, crusty-eyed hangover I'm rocking now. I more than likely need another shower, but at this point I'd kill for some takeout and a cup of Joe.

Ian left last night before I got out of the shower, and Aidan made himself scarce in my other guestroom.

I have three guestrooms in this house, and it makes me wonder why I even bought a home this big. Unless there is a crisis, there will never be a need to fill them.

It's not like I'll get married or have kids. I don't know if children are even possible. What if I'm a sterile offspring of two species that were never meant to come together? Like a horse and a donkey making a mule. A genetic freak never meant to reproduce.

And why am I thinking about having kids? My only romantic prospect in a freaking century just walked out on me. Babies are farther away than the moon at this point.

Tired, disgruntled, and grudgingly heartbroken, I peel myself from the chair to raid the takeout drawer. Making my way to the kitchen, I pull the overfull-drawer open, rifling through the disorganized menus. There has to be a place I can call... with no phone because mine is broken into a bazillion pieces. Shit.

The back door opens, Aidan pausing at the threshold with bags in his hands. His eyes are wide, and it really isn't any guess what he's gawking at. Stained pajama pants, rat's nest hair, last night's makeup smeared under my eyes. Yeah, I know I look like a train wreck, but honestly, it's my house and I can be a mess here if I want to. Granted, he's seen me look worse, like the time I was topless with a surgical drain coming from my chest.

Yeah, I've definitely looked worse.

"Please tell me there is coffee somewhere in one of those bags." My voice is like gravel, ready to pout my lower lip if it means I can guilt him into getting me some. I'll even use tears. I'm not above it, and hey, they'll be easy to create.

He coughs to mask his chuckle, but he answers in the affirmative, so I'll allow it. "There is. Creamer too. I got a few groceries and replaced your phone. You can call to get it activated."

And now I want to cry all over again. Aidan just saved me from braving the phone store and the grocery store and the coffee shop. Swallowing hard, I manage to nod before I reach for the bags, unloading them in a hurry.

"Thanks," I murmur, but my voice is broken, as if the kindness is just a little too much, even for that single syllable. It's possible it might be.

Pulling the coffee from the bag, I set about to make us a pot, thankful for something to do.

"When you're up to it, you need to look at the warding around the property," Aidan suggests, pulling egg cartons and packages of bacon and sausage from a plastic bag. "I know you threw a band-aid one up last night, but if we're going to be here for any length of time, it's going to need to be stronger."

Nodding, I pour water into the reservoir, filling it up to the tippy-top. "I'll get on that after I start this."

I press the bright green "Start" button and hightail it

out of the room, stopping at Maria's room on the way to mine. Her eyes are still closed, but she's snoring softly, so I know she's alive. Quickly changing, not bothering to wash my face or tame my hair, I head back down the hall, through the kitchen and out the back door. Only to stop short.

Ian's sitting on one of my teak patio loungers, his ankles crossed as he stares out over the fence line to the sky beyond. He glances up at my stutter step, gives me a nod, and then looks away.

At this point I don't even want to be nice to the man, but I take the high road by not setting him on fire and resume my trek, heading for the greenhouse. I snag some pruning shears, and clip a bundle's worth of sage, careful not to cut the stalks too low. My greenhouse needs a lot of attention. Some pots are overgrown, some thirsty from the automatic drip system failing in a few places. I should have taken better care of my garden, shouldn't have let a man worth so little of my time keep me from my home.

And even though I killed him, I've somehow set him free once again.

Too many problems, not enough solutions.

Bundling the white sage with blessed twine, I hang it next to the dried bundles, the old habit of replacing what I use so ingrained, that I didn't stop to think.

I was leaving town, wasn't I?

It's not like I have a reason to stay. My shop is gone. My friends are gone, or don't want me. But even with all of that, just being in that greenhouse makes me feel better. Feeling the small spark of nature in this tiny patch of home feels like a gift—like I was given back something I lost. Nodding to myself, I step into the dry air, light the bundle of sage with a spark from my fingers, and get to work fixing the boundary to my home.

My feet rasp against the pavers as I take trudging steps up the stairs to the back door. Knowing Ian is probably only here to check on Maria doesn't take the sting out of his presence or make things any less awkward for me. But the kitchen is empty when I gather the bravery to open the back door, so my reprieve has been extended for the time being.

Hearing the television on in the living room, I make my way there, knowing out of the two brothers, Aidan is more likely to be in the living room than Ian. Aidan is watching an old movie, a black-and-white mystery I'm fond of. I say watching, but he's more like napping, his face soft, almost peaceful as he rests on the couch. I don't think he got any more sleep than I did last night, and for that I feel horrible. I softly fling the throw blanket over him, hoping the action doesn't wake him up. Nothing else to do, I head back to Maria's room to check on her.

I can't avoid Ian forever.

Ian sits at Maria's bedside, a stethoscope in his ears as he checks her heart rate or blood pressure or whatever the hell he's checking.

"How's she doing?" I break the awkward silence of Ian refusing to look at me, even though I know he knows I'm here.

"Her vitals are good. She should wake any time. Witches heal a bit faster than humans, so she may not even scar."

I'm not sure Maria would care if she did scar or not, not that the cuts to her face are grotesque —just that I don't know if my sister is vain. I don't remember her being that way, but it's been a long time.

With nothing else to say, I reply with, "Good."

Since he's taking the only seat, I rest on the edge of the bed, careful not to disturb another sleeping person in my house and take her hand. The hand itself is fine, but deep lacerations crisscross her forearms—so deep it's a wonder she kept her arm.

I hadn't noticed her right hand last night, only focusing on her left side. The wounds are closing quickly, and I don't think she'll have permanent damage, but the pain... It must have been unbearable.

Her fingers twitch in mine, and I grip them harder.

"Maria?" I call softly, not wanting to startle her. "Baby sister, you're safe. Please wake up."

Her dark-brown eyes flash open, and she frantically looks around the room. Skittering back into the headboard, she sits up, fear embedded in every line of her face until her eyes land on me.

"Maxima," she breathes. "You came for me."

"Of course I came for you. You called, didn't you?" My tone is too light for our past. Maria has never once called for my help, not since I was cast out. She never tried to go around our mother.

A part of me doesn't blame her. I wouldn't go against Teresa if I didn't have to—if it weren't ingrained in my very DNA.

Then her arms are around me, and she's crying— huge gasping sobs of a woman at the very edge of her sanity, the very end of her rope.

"Shh, Ria. You're safe. I made you safe. You're okay." I rub her back gently like I used to do when we were kids. It helps some, but she still sobs, shaking like a leaf in my arms.

"You don't know. You can't know." She says the words over and over, a faint whisper and then louder as if she's warning me away. But I do know—probably more than she does—about the dangers that once lurked in that building.

"Try me, Ria. I found you, remember? I know exactly what was in that building."

Maria pulls out of my hug, wiping her eyes and nose with a handkerchief Ian unearths from his back pocket. Since when did this man have a fucking handkerchief? Did I drink myself into a stupor and he became an adult overnight? I try not to frown at the scrap of white fabric, and watch my sister's face instead, ignoring the man beside me.

"A man came for Mama. Walked right through our wards as if it were nothing. He wanted to talk to Mom, but she was so mad at him. Not that I blame her. They talked but she shooed me out of the room like I was a child. I'm less than a decade shy of four hundred and she shoos me out of the room. I got pissed off and left them alone. Then, when I was on the stairs, I heard a boom, and the whole place shook. I thought the building was going to come down on us. The stairs collapsed, and I went through wood." She pauses, gesturing to her right arm where the damage is the worst. "Landed on the bottom floor. Then something cut me again. I couldn't see what it was... But it was big, Maxima. So big, so strong, it threw me across the room."

"A Corax demon," I supply, to her bewilderment.

I may have looked through all of my grimoires last night to find the devil bird, but I found him. It was in the one grimoire I should have looked in first, since it was a Demonology text from Gramma. But I was drunk and not thinking straight when I started.

"A what?"

"That's what attacked you. Be happy you couldn't see it in the flesh, little sister." I try and fail to suppress a shudder. "Head of a crow, body of a man, legs of a stag. Invisible to all Ethereals and humans except for ones of demon lineage. And it smelled like rotting meat. That for sure wasn't in the textbooks."

Maria looks horrified.

"Is that thing still out there?" Hysteria begins to rise in her voice.

"No. I took care of it. It is very, very dead. Do you remember anything else?"

She nods and continues with her story. "I managed to get up, but th-the Corax thingy kept throwing me. I managed to make it back to the living room—back to Mom, but then the man grabbed her and took her."

"Who was the man? Did he have a name? Can you describe him?"

"I don't need to describe him. I know who he was. Andras. Your dad took her."

I figured as much.

15

MAX

"Don't do anything stupid, Max."

I can't believe he has the gall to say that to me. In my own house, in this room, in front of my sister. Like yesterday didn't happen. Like he didn't just throw me out like garbage. Like him refusing to even look at me, but still thinking he can tell me what to do.

Fuck. That.

Without a thought, I snap my fingers, the skin of his lips melting away and turning into one piece of flesh with no opening. I snap them again, and his butt parks in the chair, his back slamming into the upholstered wingback.

I sniff and don't spare him a glance but catch him

trying to struggle from my hold out of the corner of my eye.

Maria's eyes go wide before she curls her lips into her mouth. Either from trying not to laugh or to discourage me from doing the same to her.

I turn my cold stare to him. "Don't. Tell me. What to do," I threaten through gritted teeth, seething in the wrath I've held back for far too long.

Surprise lashes through his face, and I realize he doesn't know this side of me. He doesn't know how much care I took not to hurt him, not to hurt the people around me. To fit in and be welcomed. He doesn't know how vengeful I can be or how far I've gone in my long life.

He doesn't understand what being a Rogue really means. Doesn't get that I have been used and abused, left behind in the ashes, scraping by with nothing but my grit and will to survive.

But I've always had my freedom. Always.

And I won't be told what to do.

I give him five more seconds and snap my fingers again. His lips returning to their original shape, he parts them to speak, but I cut him off.

"I have no intention of doing anything stupid. I have no intention of doing anything at all. Andras wants Teresa? They can work it out by themselves. I have no interest in what my parents need to hash out. I'm only pissed they left Maria behind. Now that she's here safe, it's not my business. Clear?"

"Crystal," he murmurs, and once again he won't look me in the eye. I'm really starting to hate that.

I snap my fingers again, letting him up from the chair, and he doesn't hesitate to get the hell out of the room. At least he's smart.

"Do I want to know why you disfigured that guy to prove a point?" Maria asks, the mirth in her voice shoving bricks of pain off my heart.

I think about it, debating whether or not I want to get into the whole Ian situation with her. "Nope. You mad?"

"Why again would I be mad at you?" She seems genuinely confused, and I hate to be the one to break it to her that when she came to me for help, I only ever intended to help *her*. Not Mom.

"I wasn't lying to Ian. I won't go look for Mom." A thread of shame skirts through me as I say the words.

"I would never expect you to." She grabs my hand. "That would *never* be your job."

She sounds compassionate, but there is a thread of something else. Something that just doesn't sound like Maria being Maria. I blink at her, surprised that she sounds… like she knows what happened.

No. She knows *exactly* what happened to me.

"You know why I was kicked out, don't you?" I don't intend it to sound like an accusation, but it does all the same. She knows more about what I went through—maybe from my mother's own mouth.

She knows. And I don't.

Maria's face would be a mask of pity if she had any for me, but that was never how my little sister rolled. Her heart hurts for me, and I almost don't want to know what it is she's about to say.

But the other part of me prays it's a good reason. Craves that it's something I can forgive my mother for. Hopes beyond hope, that for once, I'll feel even an ounce of love from my mother—even tangentially.

"And it wasn't for breaking a ward, either. Mom did it to keep you safe. To keep you out of the Royal Court and away from your family. If you were Rogue, they couldn't accept you, couldn't pull you into the fold, so the first time you messed up…" She trails off, sympathy in her every expression.

I want to cry, but my mouth forms a smile instead, even though tears fill my eyes. This is so much worse than I thought.

"She tanked my life to save it?" I chuckle, but it's a laugh of disbelief.

"I'm not saying she did the right thing. Hell, when I

found out I almost went to the Witch Conclave to have your status reinstated. But she told me who your family is, told me exactly who they are. Trust me when I say, you may prefer your Rogue status after all."

"I guess I won't know, now will I?" I shrug, wiping the stubborn tears that refused to stay confined, trying to pass it off as if it doesn't burn through my gut in the worst way.

"So why did you call me? Don't you guys have a houseful of minions at your disposal?" I ask in a roundabout way what the hell they are doing in my city in the first place.

"Not anymore. Not after what happened last year," she murmurs, reminding me of the massacre in their coven home. Last year a pair of witch siblings and their ilk ripped through the witch world, slaughtering coven leaders in an attempted coup.

While some of my blood family survived, many didn't.

"You guys didn't beef up security?"

"We did, but it isn't like they travel with us. We employ other Ethereals, too. Shifters and wraiths. But we came here on witch business. It wasn't prudent to take security with us. We thought we could handle it on our own. We thought wrong." Her hand trembles as she wipes her mouth.

"Are you hungry? I'm not much of a cook, but I make a mean breakfast."

Her shaking stops, and a smile emerges from the fear lining her face. "That would be great, thank you."

"You're full of shit," Maria says as she shovels another forkful of French toast in her mouth.

I take another sip of my coffee. "What?"

"Not much of a cook, huh? I thought I was getting toast and butter not cinnamon French toast with blueberry compote and sausage links."

She also got German potatoes and biscuits, but I can't take credit for those. I didn't make them from scratch. "What? Aidan bought me groceries. I didn't want to waste them."

"I'm not complaining," Aidan says around a mouthful of food. "But explain the takeout menus to me. I thought this food was going to rot in your fridge. Instead, I get the best breakfast I've had in a while. But don't tell Aurelia I told you that or she'll kill me."

Shrugging, I set down my coffee mug, collecting the forks and butter knives, stacking them on top of my plate. "I work too much, and I work late hours. I don't want to cook food at midnight when I finally get off. Those are all the places that deliver until two."

I collect the plates, setting them into the sink and starting the water. It's almost comforting to have people in my house, sitting at my table. Feeding them. It's been so long since I've had that. It relieves the burn in my gut that I've had since Striker left, even though I was the one who told him to go. It does nothing to cure Ian's absence, but that's a whole other wound to heal.

"Where did you—" Maria begins, but her words are stolen from her by a blast in my living room. I feel it in my bones, in my teeth, through every tissue in my body.

That blast is every single one of my wards breaking at once, snapping against my flesh like a whip. At least this time they don't break my skin. Not like last time when Micah was the one breaking through them.

Once I catch my breath, I run to the living room, wanting to see who is ballsy enough to blast their way into my home. But it isn't a person at all. It's a silvery orb of light. From the light steps a specter of a man—not a ghost, but a reproduction like a recorded message.

I've seen a few of these, but not for some time. Manifestation Lights. It was something used in olden times when one wanted to send a message but didn't want to travel. Obviously, it predated the telephone, and I haven't seen one done in at least a century. Maybe two.

How someone could bust through my wards for a message boggles my mind. The man turns in a circle, the spell seeking the recipient before the message will start. He's tall, with long dark-brown hair past his shoulders, his face scruffy as if he's deciding whether or not to grow out a beard. A scar bisects his left eyebrow, cutting high on his forehead and ending mid-cheek. His eyes, though, they are what sets him apart. They aren't hazel or brown, but a piercing glowing gold that can never pass off as human. Even in this grayed-out form, they search, their power flowing through the room, even though this is nothing more than a trumped-up recording.

Something about them niggles at my brain, but those glowing orbs finally find me, and he begins to speak.

"Daughter. I have taken your mother from you. Give me the bone blade and I will return her unharmed. Fail, and I will not be as generous. Don't make me ask twice."

So, this is Andras.

His voice is calm and succinct British, and just like any other absentee dad, he knows nothing about me. If he knew anything at all about me, he would have taken Maria instead of my mother. He would have known there is exactly zero things I would do for Teresa Alcado.

Maria, however, is a whole other story.

The message fades, the silvery orb winking out of my

living room much the same as it came in. I fight the urge to shrug and continue on with my life, because while I loathe our mother, Maria seems to still love her despite all her many, many faults.

That and a muttered "meh" would be considered rude.

Everyone else in the room stands frozen, like they're waiting for me to freak or issue orders or something. I skirt them both, heading back to the kitchen and start the dishes, ignoring them and their stares completely.

"That's it? Your dad breaks through your wards, informs you he'll hurt your mom to get what he wants, and you're just going to do the dishes?" Aidan asks, incredulous.

I squeeze the dish soap on the scrubby sponge and start attacking the now-cool griddle. "Yep."

"Wow. You really hate your mother, don't you?"

I think about it for a second. Do I hate Teresa? Maybe, but more, I'm indifferent. She's all but admitted hating the fact that my father left her. Hates that I look like him—even though I can't really see a resemblance. Maria said that she threw me out of the coven to save me, but I just can't see her lifting a finger to do me a favor. Every favor from Teresa has consequences. Every single one. Take the bone blade for example. I had to ask for it, beg for it, even. And what has that blade brought me? Nothing but pain and a personal poltergeist that I have to figure out how to kill.

Again.

I can't say I hate her. But love her? Want her safe and unharmed? Want to stick my neck out to help her, even though it would surely earn me not a stitch of gratitude in return?

Yeah, no. Hard pass.

"I don't hate her," I finally respond, not turning to look at him. "I just don't care about her. He should have picked a better bargaining chip."

Water sluices the suds off the griddle, and I arrange it in the drainer so it won't fall out.

Suddenly, all the windows in my kitchen crack at once, the glass making an audible creak before it shatters, blowing into the room like shrapnel.

Now what?

16

MAX

My fingers make a bloody smear on the white of my kitchen cabinets as I pull myself from my defensive crouch. Ears ringing, I glance around the room, the edges of it fading in and out. Aidan's down, Maria at his side, her jean-covered knees in the glass as she tries to rouse him.

In the fading daylight, it's harder to see, but the source of the trouble is a face I know well. In the dark, he was gray—somewhat solid. But in the light, his specter is barely there. I have a barely tangible hope that he's somehow fading away, but even I know my luck isn't that good.

I reach behind me where I feel nothing but an empty sheath, and I take my eyes off Micah to search the floor for my athame. This is a mistake. Micah doesn't care about a wounded wraith or my sister. He doesn't pay them any mind at all.

All he wants is me and my pain.

When I look up again, he's right there, pinning me against the counter, his icy hands once again burning my flesh through my long-sleeved shirt.

"I should thank your daddy for breaking your wards. Maybe after I'm done with you, I'll hunt him down and give him a big kiss," he whispers, the words hissing on each "s" like a snake. Fangs rake my neck, their frigid points not breaking the skin, but digging in all the same.

He won't bite me again, knowing he can't drink, can't consume me like he would his other victims, but he wants to. I can feel it. I was unaware ghosts could get stiffies, but here we are.

I'm afraid to even murmur a spell, knowing the pressure of my throat merely swallowing could cause the fangs to pierce the skin. I'm stuck. Pinned. Weaponless. Helpless.

"*I exilium sive spectra*," Maria calls, the red glow of her magics high in the air. It doesn't do much against Micah, but pulls him back just enough so I can move.

The light catches the silver of the athame, and I dive for it, cutting myself on broken glass to get it.

I don't throw it this time, instead I keep my hand on the hilt, slashing at Micah, driving him back, out of my kitchen. The blade slices his flesh, but it doesn't seem to really hurt him, just spilling silvery blood on my glass-covered floor. I try punching, but my fist only finds air, so unlike when he touches me.

Well, that's just unfair.

I move to slash again, but Micah spins, shimmering out of the way and appearing three feet from where he was standing? Floated? Do ghosts really stand?

I whisper the words my sister called, *"I exilium sive spectra."* *To banish a ghost.* A little on the nose, but I'd never begrudge Maria a spell that's working in a pinch. My power is greater than Maria's ever could be. Not hating on my sister, but her blood is pure witch, and she's a moon witch at that. There is no way Maria could have my power at dusk except for the three days of the full moon, and even then, it would take a full coven of witches to do what I can.

Sometimes demon blood has its privileges.

This time Micah skids back, his body losing its spectral balance and he rakes his hands across the floor, looking for purchase as if he's forgotten he's dead, all the while he curses me. Yelling at me every single thing he'll do to me.

I want to murmur the words again, but something in his cursing perks my ears up.

"You think I'm your only enemy? You think I'm the

only one who wants you to burn? That blonde bitch who sent me after you? She's watching you. Always watching you. You'll never find peace. I'll make sure of that."

It's the blonde bitch comment that snags my attention. I only know one blonde bitch.

"*Immobilis exspiravit.*" I snap my fingers. "What blonde. Who sent you to me?"

Micah's face is frozen in his expression of rage, but his eyes dance as if he knows he can't speak while under this spell and removing it will set him free.

I am so going to regret this.

"*Exspiravit mobilis,*" I mutter, and he *moves*, launching himself at me like a sprinter hearing the starting pistol, ready to tackle me if he has to.

Splaying my fingers just so, I press the rune on the underside of the hilt, the athame springing into its true length, and I swing just like Aidan taught me, catching Micah under his left arm. If he were alive, that swing would have taken his arm off, but since he's a ghost it only makes him howl at me.

And then I'm not standing in front of Micah. I've been yanked away, spinning from the momentum as Ian takes my place. I didn't see him get here, I didn't hear him, but here he is fighting a battle I didn't ask him to fight. I wish I could be mad at him, but I can't.

Unlike me, Ian can touch Micah, and he does.

Gripping Micah's neck, Ian shakes a rattling totem at him. The top of the totem is made from an animal's skull—a bird of some kind, possibly a raven or crow, but I've had enough of those animals to last a lifetime, so I hope not. The rest is feathers and a carved wooden handle, engraved with sigils I've only seen in my French Creole grimoires that freak me way the hell out.

Ian's speaking an old bastardized French Creole, a dialect I haven't heard before, so I have no fucking idea what he's saying. But Micah does. He's screaming obscenities at him, cursing him and his children, promising vengeance in all its forms.

But one word catches my attention.

Messorem. Harvester. Reaper.

"Don't kill him." The ache of Micah's touch is seeping into my bones. "Someone sent him after me when he was alive. I want to know who."

Ian's chanting stops, the shaking of the totem along with it, but his hand at Micah's throat is like a vice.

"The question isn't who sent me to you. The question is who pulled the angel's strings to send a demon to your door," he rasps. "Think about that."

A blonde bitch who is also an angel? *Yeah, I only know one of those.* Rage courses through me, but by a force of will, I manage to choke it back.

"Ruby sent you to me. Did she happen to inform you why?"

Micah smiles, loving the banked rage shining in my eyes. "I didn't ask."

"Then you're of no use to me."

Micah's eyes go wide, fear in their grayed-out pools. He struggles, shoving at Ian, managing to catch him under the chin and Ian's hand loses its grip. Micah doesn't waste what is likely his only opportunity to escape. The house rumbles as he fades out, the glass levitating from the floor before exploding outward once again.

I don't come out unscathed. Ten or twenty shards of glass are embedded into the arm I used to cover my face and neck. Even more are entrenched like darts in my cabinets and walls. Maria and Ian have a few, but I seem to have taken the brunt of Micah's rage.

Lucky me.

Aidan picks that moment to startle awake, just as his brother is checking him over.

If Micah's little attack has taught me anything, it's that I need to get my wards back up—and pronto.

"Maria, can you cast?" I want to get in the yard before the sun goes down. The last thing I need is to try warding this place in the dark.

She looks up from Ian's hands as he checks his

brother's vitals, her eyes a shocky kind of wide I know all too well.

"Y-yeah. I can cast."

Giving her something to do will help us both, and maybe, just maybe, I'll be able to figure out why the hell Ruby sent Micah to me. "Good, follow me. We need to re-ward this place now."

"I have plywood in the garage. See what you can make work if you can't repair the back door. This place needs to be secure and now," I tell Ian, earning me a terse nod in response.

He might have thought I created this kind of havoc on my own, but Micah's confession is proof positive that someone started this mess, and it wasn't me.

Maria follows me out the back door, into the greenhouse where I pick up my smudge stick.

"Is this all you're warding with? A smudge stick?"

I look from the burnt end of the smudge stick and back to her. Her eyes are incredulous, mouth a grim line. "What else am I supposed to use?"

A strangled sort of croak falls from her lips. "No wonder people have been breaking your wards left and right, big sister. You suck at warding. Let me show you how it's done." She brushes by me and my puny sage, snagging my pruning shears on the way.

I guess I'm about to get schooled by my little sister.

Warding her way is complicated. And takes about a bazillion ingredients—luckily, I have them all, but Fates, she has a laundry list of crap. Stones, fetishes, and so much salt. Seriously, she might make quarries go out of business.

"And then we're supposed to set it all on fire?" It may or may not be my fifth time asking.

I've done wards so complex even Aurelia can't get visions through them. So airtight wraiths can't feel their mates through them. So badass cell signals won't work. I have never, not once used a single stone, rose petal, or bird feather in any of them.

But I don't tell her that.

"Yeah. One at each corner of your home."

"Well, that will go over well with the neighbors," I mutter, but do as she says, arranging a bowl at the northern point, light it on fire, and move to the next one, trailing a line of salt from one to the next.

"I know you think your way is better, but if you have ghosts after your ass, you might want to try it my way— just for a little while. Your way keeps out living things. Not dead things."

Okay, so she has a point.

I move to the next and the next, setting a small bowl of blessed oils, dried herbs, feathers, and rocks on the raised retaining wall surrounding my property. Fucking rocks. Do rocks even burn?

"Point taken."

She takes a deep breath as if she's gearing up for something. Then she lets it rip.

"I want you to at least consider trying to find Mom," she says in a rush, as if she wants to get all the words out before I say no. She used to do the same thing when we were kids.

Pursing my lips, I pretend to think about it. "I'm not giving up the blade."

"And I don't expect you to. But if we don't find her, Andras might kill her. I know you don't like her, but Mom is really important to our coven and to the American covens. Losing her would be a blow."

"I know someone who might be able to help us, but she's not going to like us coming to her with this any more than I like having to ask her." I try to warn Maria before she gets her hopes up.

In all likelihood, Bernadette isn't going to help us. Not once she finds out who took Mom and what he wants in exchange. But she's crafty enough that she just might put aside her duty and help me. Even if it's to deceive her son.

"I'll take it."

17

MAX

"You have got to be shitting me."

Maria has said this at least four times since we started on the trek to Bernadette's cabin in the valley, walking the two-point-three miles in the dark. I don't tell her we probably could have traveled here, and trying not to laugh at her is likely going to give me a hernia. I say "probably" on the travel bit because I have no idea what kind of booby traps Gramma has set up in this place, and I'm really not willing to find out.

I've got juice, but Bernadette, AKA Lilith, AKA all hail the Queen, AKA the baddest bitch in Hell, has *juice*. I don't know if she has traps or if she even thinks it's pertinent to set any, but I'm not going to piss her off if I don't have to.

Just like the last time, it's pitch dark when we make

it to the trailhead, which looks out onto a ninety-degree cliff and the valley below. And just like last time, there is no way on this earth or any other I'm belaying down that bitch.

I look over the cliff, the moonlight catching the tips of the razor-sharp rocks just right, and start busting up laughing, unable to hold back any longer.

"Yeah, there is no way we're climbing down there. We travel from here. It's the reason I brought Aidan."

Well, that and Ian refused to come. He hasn't said much to me since he decided to end things, unless it's to try and tell me what to do.

"I can't take you, but Aidan can. But the ride is going to suck, so don't bitch out and puke, deal?" The last thing she'll want to do before meeting who we're meeting is to puke right before the introductions.

"Fine. How bad could it be?"

Famous last words, little sister. I think those words and manage not to say them, which is good, because the veil between what I think and what I say is usually pretty thin. I only manage a shrug, and then snap my fingers, landing in the stream again, soaking my Chuck's and startling a falcon on a nearby tree branch. Its feathers ruffle as it shrieks at me.

Sorry, bird.

Grumbling, I snatch my flashlight from my pack,

signaling to them that it's safe and to give Aidan a visual marker of where to land. Not a second later, Aidan and Maria are in the stream, and Maria is trying not to gag. I pass over my water bottle so she doesn't heave.

"Fates, that is awful." She sucks down more water to wash away the likely heaviness on her tongue.

Been there.

"Okay, like I said. Be nice. Don't be an asshole, and wipe your feet. I'm going to knock on the ward. Don't go ahead of me and cross. I have absolutely no idea what that thing will do." I leave out the part where it won't hurt me because I'm a blood relative.

Them, however…

I gently tap-tap-tap on the pale luminescent hex lines of the ward and wait. Not ten seconds later, the door pops open, and Bernadette flies out of the cabin.

"Maxima, dearie, I've missed you. I was afraid you'd hate me after that whole blade nonsense." She rushes, stopping only when she notices I'm not alone. "Oh! You've brought guests. Come in, come in. I have brownies just out of the oven."

Bernadette gestures to Aidan and Maria to head in, but Maria stops and whispers in my ear before she passes me, "She isn't going to fatten us up and eat us, is she? Because Grimm fairy tales are there for a reason."

I bite my lip to keep from giggling and pray

Bernadette didn't hear her. I shake my head "no" and give my sister big eyes. The ones that say she's going to get us in trouble. Maria got "big eyes" a lot when we were kids. Half the times I was reprimanded for being insolent, Maria was the one who made me laugh.

"Bernadette, this is my friend, Aidan, and my sister, Maria."

Bernadette takes each of their hands in turn, clasping their right hands in both of hers. She's smiling while she does it, but her eyes take a far-off quality that makes me wonder what she really sees. Does she see the future like Aurelia? Does she see the past like she did with me?

Or does she see possibilities?

I suppose I'll never know unless I ask her, but now isn't the time for that conversation.

"It seems you never visit me with good news, Maxima, and never at a more reasonable hour. Are you nocturnal? Some of us are like that," she offers, not unkindly.

"No... well, I might be. When my tattoo shop was still standing, I worked until midnight most nights, and didn't typically get home until two a.m." I say it offhandedly, but Gramma's eyes narrow at my use of the word "was" in reference to my shop.

She presses her lips together as she gestures to a light-colored sofa and a pair of chintz chairs offering us a place to sit. "Yes, well, we know who is responsible for that, don't we? I had no idea he would go after you so quickly, dear. I had no idea he even had the thought in his head."

She's referring to Andras, but everything about how things have played out in the last few days makes no sense. Why tear down my wards only to leave the safe behind? Why attack my shop? Was it to get the blade from the safe? And if it was, why use my mother as bait? Why not strike me once it was out?

And Ruby.

I'd guessed it was her, but I didn't know for sure. Micah never said her name specifically.

"I know you didn't, but there is something we need to talk about."

"Of course, dear." She sweeps her hand in the air in a circular motion, then snaps her fingers. A full tea service appears on the coffee table. "Drink your tea. It's a nice oolong."

I take a teacup and a cucumber sandwich, nibbling on the end more from nerves than actual hunger.

I've never actually seen Bernadette pissed off before, and well, if there was anything to take a normally genial person straight to the edge, it's family bullshit.

"Andras sent me a message." I pause, waiting for her to digest what I just said. I can't imagine what she must be feeling. One of her sons killed the other. To be in this position in and of itself must be torture. "He has my mother and wants the bone blade in exchange for her."

"No." The clink of her teacup hitting the saucer is slight but still makes me jump.

I spare a glance at Maria, and her eyes fill at the abrupt denial. "I understand your position, but could you tell me why he wants it? If he killed Samael, then he already has something that will kill a demon. He doesn't need the blade. So why is he going through so much trouble to get it?"

Bernadette sighs and relaxes her rigid posture, leaning back on the cushions. "Because he can? Because he's killed with it before? I made that blade ages ago in a very dark time in my life. Hell had just been made, and our tasks there made me frightened of what I would become. Hell is a place for punishment, and demons are the punishers. We were chosen by the Fates to dole out our power only to the most wicked, and at first it seemed righteous. But as the years went on... I couldn't separate myself from the punishment I gave. I made the blade and the spell, but I never married them. And when my husband started hurting people not remanded to Hell, hurting my children, myself, started talking of war with the angels, I gave my son the blade and Teresa the spell. Your father killed my husband. Not necessarily at my request, but he had my help. The blade I planned on using to kill myself took my husband's life. That blade might not be the only one with the power to kill a demon, but it is the only one that can remand a soul, taking the soul's power for itself."

It takes a full minute to digest what she's saying. The blade that currently sits at my hip killed my grandfather and however many it took to get to him.

And that wasn't even its real purpose.

"Why did you make it so it would take the soul?"

"Because I feared with all I'd done, with all the punishment I gave, I wouldn't be worthy of the Otherside. I would go back to Hell, and I would rather be trapped in a vast nothingness than go back to that place. Spirits that have been housed inside it seek it for its silence."

A weight heavier than I would have expected settles on my heart.

I freed them.

All of them.

All of those souls.

"The break. It let them all out. Some have already come for me. Micah in particular. He said someone sent him to me—when he was alive. A blonde angel. I worry that the person who sent him to me is Ruby." Admitting this out loud is something that could get me killed. The demon-angel no-touch rule is serious. I have no doubt that if it's proven Ruby did send Micah to me it could violate the Armistice.

"If it was Ruby, then the Council will let it go. She got a demon to do her dirty work for her, that's how we've dealt with our enemies for eons—by getting someone on their side to pull a little friendly fire. Plus, dear, I hate to remind you, but you're a Rogue. No Council member could rule on the side of a Rogue, and you know it as well as I do. I don't like it, but I can't change it. I can't start the war that will end this world for just one person—even if that person is you, dearie. I'm sorry for that, but it's the truth."

I know it isn't intended to feel like a slap, but it does. Although I know why she feels this way, it still stings a little, even though in no way do I want the world to end just because Ruby is a dick.

It's the indifference that really hurts.

"I can accept that. She'll at least lose her job, right? I'm all for the world not ending, but she shouldn't have as much power or be as close to someone with power as she is if she's sending out demon kill squads. And moreover, why, though? Why me? I didn't even know her name when Micah came to me. Why send him my way when I'd never even met the woman?"

"I suppose I'll make sure Caim asks her." Her reply is

curt, and I fear she's leaving something out. Like she's keeping something from me. Everything about her answers just haven't seemed right at all.

Nothing about this night is right.

It takes a full minute of silence before Aidan stands —having said almost nothing since he got here, he only nods in deference to Bernadette, and walks right out the door. The line of his shoulders vibrates in anger, and while I'd like to think it's on my behalf, I know it probably isn't.

I'm a Rogue. Why should I expect anyone to really give a shit about me? Even family.

Maria manages a polite, "Excuse me," before she follows suit.

"I know you'll do what you think is right, Maxima, but giving him that blade will surely mean all of our deaths. You must see that."

I stand, skirting the low coffee table and pressing a kiss to her forehead. I do see how giving up the blade could mean my death, but it makes me wonder how much of a stain I'll have on my soul if I don't.

I attempt to rise when Bernadette reaches for the sheath that holds the bone blade, her fingers latching onto the hilt before the spell that keeps it safe slams her back. Her face is awash in shock with threads of anger and a little bit of shame, but I can feel nothing but disappointment.

Disappointment and disillusionment.

Like I'd been robbed when I thought I had nothing to steal.

"I would have given it to you if you'd only asked."

Rising, I turn my back on my grandmother and walk out.

Once I follow Aidan and Maria outside the wards, the pain ripping a hole in my chest only growing worse as I leave Bernadette behind.

Toeing off my Chuck's, I walk in the pitch-black stream, the water cool on my feet as I stare up at the clear sky. Stars—so many and so vast—sprinkle the night sky with just enough beauty to keep me going.

Just enough goodness to wash a little of the hurt away.

I don't look at my sister, and I don't look at Aidan. I can feel their eyes on me as I make this decision—the one I don't want to make but have to.

"Okay, I'm in. Let's go get her."

18

MAX

What does one wear when they go off on a quest to kill their father? I ponder this as I try to decide between a 1960s mod-style wiggle dress and a pair of gray skinny jeans, thick leather boots, and a tank top that says "Sunshine and Fucking Rainbows" in a circle surrounding a skull and crossbones.

I know which one will be more comfortable should the evening not go according to plan, and I know which one will irritate my mother the most. Spoiler alert: they're the same outfit, and that thought makes me smile.

It really is the little things.

Getting dressed, I make sure the sheath at my spine

is secure and adjust the weapons so they can lay right under my jacket. Walking down the hall, I hear the brothers arguing in the living room, their voices carrying through the house.

"You're going to get her killed. You're going to get yourself killed. You didn't even want me to be a part of this, and now you're what, just along for the ride? What the fuck, Aidan?" There is a thud of flesh hitting flesh, but only once and no more.

I hear Aidan whisper, but I can't quite make out what he's saying. I'd hate for someone—*cough, Maria, cough* —to catch me in this hallway eavesdropping, so I quit my hiding and walk into the kitchen.

Maria is sitting at the table, a bottle of bourbon in one hand and a glass in the other, listening to the guys bitch at each other from the safety of the breakfast nook.

"...I'm not the one who threw her away, brother. That's all on you." Aidan's deep growl is clear as a fucking bell even from in here, and I turn my eyes from the hallway leading to the living room to my sister. Her expression likely mirrors my own, eyes wide, mouth gaping open like a fish.

Maria starts snickering first, and then I follow, busting up laughing for I have no idea why. I'm not even sure I want to know why—at least not right now.

All I know is it keeps me from thinking Ian would rather I go alone than have help, and I keep laughing to make sure that particular hurt doesn't stick its barb right in my heart.

Once my laughter dies down, I focus on Maria. She has emptied that glass twice since I came in the room, and I wonder if I should be worried.

"You mad?"

She focuses on me—a little drunkenly, but I'll take it. "Why would I be mad at you? I know why you don't want me to go"—She raises her glass—"I'm a liability."

She can't quite mask the hurt in her voice, though, and that really sucks.

"Baby girl, you aren't a liability. I have every faith you can hold your own. You are strong and capable, and a fucking badass. But you're my weakness. If Andras had taken you, there would have been nothing I wouldn't have done to get you back. If he takes you now, I won't be able to kill him. I won't be able to do anything but get you back."

Her eyes mist over, and she takes another sip of bourbon. "Even though you got left behind?"

"Even then." I tilt down to kiss her forehead. "Always."

"But you'll have my brother out there with you." Ian's voice lashes the air behind me.

"Yes, and you'll be here protecting my sister. Even-Steven."

Ian levels me with a glare that could cut glass. "You'll bring him back."

"Or die trying."

"That's what I'm afraid of."

We manage to track Andras—or rather my mother—to Savannah. Savannah is a witch "hub," of sorts. The Southeast Coven leader even has a home here. I'd met her once after she'd been attacked in said home, nearly all of her security taken out on the same day my mother and sister were attacked.

That wasn't a great time to be a witch leader.

The locator spell tagged my mother in the middle of the historic district, and I'd taken great pains to map out the area since I was in no way familiar with the city.

I tend to stay out of witch hubs.

"You sure you want to be here?" Aidan asks under his breath as we traverse a sidewalk of the canopied street. Savannah is known in some circles as "spook central" with its ghost tours and such. A lot of battles were won and lost here, a lot of dead, and not just old dead. I assume just like in Denver, the veil is thin here, and there has been enough death, enough blood soaked into the ground to power the ley lines until the end of time.

"No, I don't want to be here. At least if we run into a spook, you can eat him. What the hell am I going to do? Stab at him? Make him run away? I swear to the Fates this place is creepy." I try and fail to suppress a full-body shudder.

"I meant with your parents." Aidan gives me a sideways glance like I must be some special form of stupid.

"Oh."

"Yeah, *oh*."

"Honestly, I'm almost four hundred. I should be over my parental issues by now, right?"

Aidan stops walking. "Why should your age have anything to do with it? They're your parents, and they failed you."

Unable to give him a good answer, I simply shrug and keep walking, leaving him to trail behind me. My mother is in one of the dozens of houses that border Forsyth Park, and I won't know which one until we get a bit closer.

Maria spelled one of my rose-quartz crystals to get hotter the closer I was to her, which is fine in theory, but only works if you're really close.

"Anything yet?"

"A general warmness. Let's get closer to the spot I pegged on the map and see if this thing actually works. It's not like I can just keep an eye out for warding lines. This place has magic out the ass, almost every house is lighting up like a damn Christmas tree."

Witch hubs. It's no wonder I picked Denver as my home. Shifters and angels roam those parts. Sure, there are a few witches thrown in, but they tend to stay in cities with a bigger base of power like New Orleans, Savannah, and Boston.

Forsyth Park is all but deserted, there are a few people out giving Fido his last stroll, a few revelers still cackling about a ghost tour they just took, but everyone else is smartly hanging up their hat for the night. I snap my fingers, arriving a few hundred feet away from the pin in the map, Aidan arriving beside me.

"How come you don't puke when you do that, but whenever I take you anywhere it's chunks city?"

Just thinking about it makes me want to dry heave. "Because I'm not using another species' magic?"

"But demons and wraiths aren't far off from each other. It shouldn't be that bad."

He's probably right, but then again, I'm not all demon, now am I? Shrugging, I keep a lookout for visitors. "Don't ask me. I just work here."

Moving closer, I can peg the house. To call it a mansion would be too broad a statement, and yet there is nothing else I could call it. Built probably in the 1800s, everything about the home is a work of art. From the moldings to the columns to the garden. Everything is arranged to be pleasing to the eye, and yet... That house holds two of the worst people ever created.

It's a wonder how many Ethereal families are just like mine. Where the cast-offs are always on the outside looking in.

I feel the coldness first, a freezing caress on the back of my neck. It stops me in my tracks, afraid that I've just imagined it, and even more afraid that I didn't.

"Aidan." His name is barely a breath on my lips.

"I feel it."

Trembling, I pull the athame, pressing the rune to expand the blade. The streetlights flicker, barely keeping lit under the strain of power heading for us, the city practically vibrating under my feet. What sounds like the wind howling perks up my ears. I know it isn't really the wind, even though I have a distinct hope that if someone were to peek out their window, they don't see what I am.

"What the hell is that?" Aidan shouts over the din, and I hate to have to tell him the truth.

"Souls. Hundreds, thousands. Micah brought friends."

It's a trap. Andras never wanted to exchange the knife for my mother. All he wanted was for me to get close, to leave the safety of my city and pounce like the dickhead he is. He wants the blade, but leaving me alive is just too much of a liability.

The ground vibrates hard enough to nearly shake me off my feet. I can't stop this. I can't even fight against it. I was stupid to come here in a place soaked in so much death, in a place where the dead are celebrated.

I close the distance between Aidan and me, not using him like a shield, but the fact that he's bigger than me and is a better fighter, well...

"How many souls can you eat at a time? Is it like a one by one thing, or can you unhinge your jaw like a snake?" I'm only half-kidding. I'd take a wraith with indigestion over dying in the midst of this shit any day.

Aidan peers down at me, his face awash in what I can only peg as regret. He's fighting his phase—his eyes flickering back and forth from full black to pale green. Against his will his fangs lengthen, his jaw popping and reforming. Black mist cradles him in its embrace, swirling around his legs, his arms. "I can't take them all. Sssome of them don't dessssserve to go."

His words hiss as he says them, the snake-like quality of all wraiths coming to the surface. He means to Hell. Some of them are good souls tricked into doing the bidding of someone else. After what Bernadette described of Hell, I wouldn't be able to send someone there unless they really deserved it. Meaning we could die if we stay.

Meaning we *will* die if we stay.

"Max, we need to go," he shouts, and I glance back to the house my mother is likely in. Where she's waiting for me to come get her. I promised I would do this—save her—but I also promised I would keep Aidan alive.

And I can't do both.

Aidan grabs my hand, pulling me, running farther from the house that holds my mother. I feel the lift, the pull of his wraith ability tugging on me, ripping me apart bit by bit.

Then Aidan's hand is ripped from mine, and all I feel is cold—the frigid aching burn of the clutches of a spirit. The warmth of the August night is all but gone, all that is left is cold, hard hands tearing at my hair, my skin. Micah's face appears right in front of me, and all I can do is hope Aidan got out, and he's smart enough not to come back.

"You're some kind of stupid, aren't you? Instead of staying behind those wards where I can't get to you, you come here of all places. Don't you know, Maxima? The dead have power here," he murmurs in my ear, chuckling.

I scream when he presses the tip of his freezing finger against my cheek. This time my skin doesn't just burn with a bout of frostbite. This time I can actually feel the skin cells die.

"Why? You said someone told you to go after me. Why are you still doing their bidding? You're dead!" I scream in his face, wishing he was actually corporeal so I could spit in his face too.

"You should know, Poppet, even death doesn't break a contract." He seems so pleased with himself, as if death makes no difference to him. As if he might be getting something out of the deal.

Micah's fingers latch around my throat, the burning, squeezing strength in them cutting off my breath, freezing my skin and deeper. Reaching into my body and snuffing the flame that is me. My body goes slack, and some of the cold on my arms fade away. I can't tell if it's from spirits letting me go or from shock. The tips of my boots frantically scrape the pavement, the athame falling from my loose fingertips.

In the distance, I hear Aidan's roar of frustration, of pain. Wherever he is, he's losing—the honor he clings to so fiercely is failing him this time.

I only have one weapon I can reach, and I swore I wouldn't unsheathe it unless I had to. This seems like a "have to" kind of situation. My fingers scramble for the hilt of the bone blade, pulling it free. Micah doesn't notice me moving, his once-ice-blue eyes focused more on my throat where his hands are squeezing the life right out of me.

I slash at his arm, doing anything to break the hold he has on me, and I'm rewarded with sweet air when his grip loosens and falls. Falling to my hands and knees, I take a second to catch my breath before I slash and stab at anything I can reach, the black specter of the souls swirling around the pair of us.

"He said the blade couldn't touch me anymore." Micah cradles his wrist, disbelief written all over him as he stares at the wound the blade created. Blood—black as night and twice as thick—pours from the gash in his arm.

"I guess he lied." I stagger to standing, ready to face him head-on, prepared to kill the demon who has haunted me since the day he came into my life.

Since the day he was hired to ruin me.

Micah bares his fangs to me. Forgetting his arm, he braces himself, ready to take me on. Out of the two of us, I'm definitely the worse for wear, and I don't know if I'll be able to win this time around. Micah strikes, his talons slicing through my jacket and the thin fabric of my shirt into my belly, the warm gush of my blood cooling while tainted with his spirit.

"This is how I killed Melody. Just like this," he hisses in my face, the agony of that statement worse than the killing blow he's made to my middle.

And then he's gone. I'm out of Micah's clutches and in warm arms while another man—a man made of darkness and glowing golden eyes attacks him with a sword made of pale bone. The ally flickers back and forth from human-shaped to smoke, and I recognize him.

Andras.

I don't know why he's helping us, but I can't worry too much about that right now.

Turning from the melee, I look up to see Aidan hovering over me, keeping me warm as my blood leaks from my body. He's crying, his tears carving tracks down his filth-covered face, and I don't know why. My death doesn't mean much to anyone but Aurelia and Maria, and even then, Maria's lived almost her whole life without me. Ian might care for a minute, but my death is to be expected. He won't mourn for very long.

But of all people, I would have thought Aidan would take my death in stride. The fact that he isn't is a balm on my battered soul. I want to reassure him, but I'm a little too focused on breathing to think up anything particularly profound.

"Don't wo-worry. I'll be right b-back," I mutter, the

heat and strength and life pouring from me as I struggle to drag the blade into its sheath.

"You damn well better be," he orders, guiding my fingers so I can seat the blade.

I want to tell him to be careful.

But I never get the chance.

19

AIDAN

Max's mouth parts as if she's about to tell me something when her eyes roll back in her head, and her body goes slack. Blood stains her full bottom lip like one of her lipsticks, and I feel the loss of her light like a gut punch. Shaking her, I plead for her to wake up.

But just like in our lessons, she doesn't listen to me.

I don't have much time. If I want her safe, if I want her to come back, I need to get her out of here.

"Answer me!" the man—Andras—shouts, his fingers around Micah's throat. I've never seen anyone but my brother able to touch a ghost, but Andras is. "Tell me where my brother is."

Micah's lips tip up, black blood staining his teeth in a

grotesque smile. Andras growls at him before taking Micah's head with the edge of a bone sword. How he can do that to a man that's already dead I don't know, and I don't care. I'm just sorry I didn't get to do it myself.

Andras wipes off the blade and slips it over his shoulder into a sheath draped across his back. When he sees Max, he does a stutter step, his nostrils flaring, scenting the blood. He rushes us, and my instincts kick in. I gather Max in my arms, protecting her and baring my fangs to the bastard also known as her father.

"Give me my daughter, wraith."

"Over my cold, dead body."

I know I can't beat him. I know it would be the dumbest thing I've ever done to try. But I also know there is no way I'm leaving this woman unprotected. There is no way I'm letting this man take her from me.

Not now, not ever.

"Look, I know you don't trust me, but I can save her. I can heal her. Just…" He trails off, "Just let me try, okay?"

My nostrils flare of their own accord as I take in his scent. And I feel nothing. No hunger, no thirst for the soul of an evil man.

Just nothing. It doesn't make sense. An evil man kidnaps. An evil man sends spirits to do his dirty work. An evil man orders the death of his daughter.

"You… you aren't evil." It comes out as an accusation, and it is. His scent doesn't make sense with all the wrong he's done. For all that he's taken.

"I know I'm not, but that doesn't stop people from believing it. Look, these spirits aren't going to just go away. They're drawn to the blade." He nods to the bone blade sheathed at Max's hip. The one I had to help her put away because she was too weak to do it. "We need to go inside the ward."

The screams of the swarming souls circle around us, spirits teeming, roiling to come closer but they don't.

"Why aren't they coming closer? Why don't they just attack?"

He taps the hilt of the blade across his back. "Because they know if they do, I'll cut them down. It's kind of what I'm known for."

"Fine. Lead the way." I gather Max in my arms once again and follow Andras.

I don't trust him. I probably won't ever trust a man who could leave Max behind—a man who could treat her like nothing. But I don't have to. All I need is for her to be healed, and she can drive this train when she wakes up.

If she wakes up.

I feel the burn of it when we cross the ward, and

stutter to a stop when I see a woman on the porch who wasn't there before. She looks eerily familiar.

"For Fates sake, Andras. You bring her back to me like this?" The woman reaches for Max, but I pull her away.

"I'm her mother, wraith. Give her to me."

I know all about Teresa Alcado, and I'd trust the demon with Max over this woman.

"Never." I growl with as much menace as I can muster, flashing my fangs. "Not you. Never you. She'd rather die and come back than have you touch her."

I only know this because she told me as much. Max had said those words in the middle of a session. I'd tried to piss her off, not realizing her mother was the ultimate trigger. She almost took my head off that day, and I never brought her up again.

Her mother will never touch Max on my watch. Not as long as I'm breathing. Teresa looks like I've slapped her, but I don't give a flying monkey fuck.

Andras steps in between me and Teresa, tucking her hands behind his body. "She needs my blood. We can do this inside where she'll wake up comfortable or out here, but either way she doesn't have time. She's fading."

Following him inside, I settle on a deep-seated couch with her on my lap, the blood staining the light fabric.

I'm not letting her go, and no one says a word to me telling me I can't.

Not that I'd listen.

Andras holds his hand out for a blade, and Teresa passes one over. Immediately, he slices his wrist lengthwise, pouring blood on Max's stomach. Andras even presses his fingers into the wound at his wrist and wipes some of his blood over the blackened burn on her cheek.

I watch as the wound on her face lightens, turning the pink of scar tissue before evening out to the deep tan of Max's skin. Her stomach is a whole other story. There is organ damage, tissue damage. Andras has to slice the skin of his wrist several times, draining himself to save his daughter's life.

Maybe he doesn't know how many times Max has died and come back. Maybe he doesn't think she'll come back this time. Maybe he's just trying to gain her favor.

Either way, I still don't trust the man. I'm just glad he wasn't lying about healing her.

The rest we'll deal with when she wakes up.

MAX

Rolling over in the arms of a man you have no idea you fell asleep on is hella awkward. Eyelids flashing open, I take stock. I'm looking at a throat. A very handsome throat, but a throat, nonetheless. Said throat is attached to a bearded chin. Then I lose sight of the chin because arms tighten, legs pin, and I'm stuck, plastered to a considerable man chest. I resist the urge to fondle said man chest, but the urge is strong.

Wriggling, I free a hand, pushing it between us so I can use it as a fulcrum to lever off Aidan's pecs. Sweet Fates, please don't let me start perving on Ian's brother. I seriously don't have time to deal with the drama that would come from me having a crush on my pseudo-ex's family members. No one has time for that.

Aidan's eyes flash open, and I'm crushed against said chest. Again.

"Freedom!" I yell, muffled by Aidan's shirt. Then I'm snapping my fingers and he's on the floor.

"The fuck?" he grumbles from the hardwood floor... that I've never seen before. This whole place is unfamiliar.

Peeling myself from the couch cushions, I clap eyes on my parents sitting side by side on the opposite love seat, their hands entwined.

Together.

I'm dreaming. I have to be. I've never seen my parents in the same room. Ever. I've never even met my dad, and except for a Manifestation Light, I wouldn't even know what the man looks like. My mother said she hated him, but she doesn't seem to mind him now.

Confused, I meet my mother's eyes. "Explain."

Before my mother can open her mouth, Andras starts laughing. "Fates, Essa, she's just like you."

While I'm sure he's having a good old time with his "bonding moment," comparing me to my mother is a sure-fire way to get on my bad side.

"Take that back right now." Somehow one of my green sparking fingers finds its way pointed at Andras as he keeps laughing—harder now that my ire has surfaced.

"I'm sure this whole family reunion shit is long overdue, but we have bigger problems than who resembles who. Mass of souls. Right outside the door." I lean over the side of the couch and give Aidan a grateful look, throwing a hand out to help him up since I was the one to toss him off in the first place.

"What the fuck happened, and why are we in the same room with the man who tried to have me killed?" I mutter under my breath as Aidan takes his seat next to me.

"He didn't. He saved your life. Let him talk and then we're out of here. Deal?"

Meeting his eyes, I see the honesty in them, and I can't help but give him a nod.

"A horde of spirits attacked. You were injured,

Andras saved your life." Teresa's words are succinct, but they paint a good picture of what happened.

"Thank you? But why? I'm immortal. I die, I come back, rinse, repeat. Unless someone decides to kill me with one of those bone blades, I'm unkillable. Why save me? Unless you want something."

"While I confess I do want a favor, saving you seemed like the honorable thing to do. Your mate had no qualms about it."

"He isn't my mate," I contest, and then Andras' eyes take on a weird sort of glow, bumping them up from just yellow to a luminescent golden, and I remember where I'd seen those eyes before.

The man at the ward in 1642.

"You." My voice is a low growl of indignation. "You got me burned at the stake. You were the man trapped at the ward. You made me save you."

At least he has the good sense to look ashamed. "I never meant for that to happen. Fates, this is such a mess. Can we start over? Hi, I'm Andras, your dad. I'm known in most circles as a gigantic ass, but I'm a delightful person once you get to know me."

I play along. "Nice to meet you. I'm Max, your daughter. I'm a Rogue because you forced me to take down a ward that protected my entire coven, which got me burned at the stake. Great. We've done the introductions. What's it going to take to get my mother out of your clutches?"

"I was looking for you," he lies.

"You were looking for the bone blade you had my mother hide. Try again."

Andras explodes, standing from the couch as if he has the right to be angry with me. "She wasn't hiding you well enough! My family was coming to look for you. So…"

Realization dawns and I find my feet. "So, you worked together to tank my life. You two set me up. How did you even know I would survive? Huh? Did that even cross your minds? Did you even care?"

"We knew you would survive," Teresa whispers, tears gathering in her eyes. "You died once, on the crossing from Spain. I held you in my arms for two days, hoping you would come back to me. On the second day you drew breath again as if you were never sick, and I knew you were more like your father than me. It was the last time you were ever ill."

That only takes away a minor facet of the pain. All this trouble to get me out of the family line, but who in the family is left?

"Your father is dead. Your brother is dead. Your

mother has been relatively decent to me. Who are you keeping me from that you haven't already killed?"

"You speak of what you can't possibly know. I didn't kill Samael."

"Then who did?"

"No one. He isn't dead."

20

MAX

No one. *He isn't dead.*

Then what the hell am I doing here? Why would the Council order Andras' death if he hadn't just killed his brother? Why would they send me to kill him if he'd done nothing wrong?

"Then why does the Council want you dead?" Aidan asks the question that has been brewing inside my head for the last few minutes.

Andras seems as if he is being overly taxed by having to explain the current mess we're all in. "He faked his death with the help of one of the Council's minions. They believe he is dead. He's trying to pin the murder on me to keep me out of the Council seat."

"And how is that going to work? He pins the murder on you, you get killed, and then he what? Just shows back up with a 'Just kidding!' act and no one's the wiser? I smell bullshit."

Andras chuckles as if I've said something cute. "He doesn't plan for there to be a Council at all. He wants me out of the way so he can murder them one by one and start the bloody war. You know, the one that will happen when a demon kills an angel?"

"Then why pin it on you at all?"

"Payback for killing our father, most likely. It's a way to drive me out of hiding so he can keep me out of the way. He plans to kill our mother *and* every other Council member *and* their second. I'm the diversion."

And I thought my drama with Teresa was bad. I can thoroughly attest that as bad as it got with us, at least I never plotted her murder.

"So, was it you who burned down my tattoo shop or your brother?"

"Samael. He knew you had the blade"—He nods at the bone knife in its sheath—"He needed it out in the open."

"I kinda wish he would have tried to open that safe. It would have saved us all a lot of time. Let me guess, you need it to kill him. Why this blade? Isn't there another weapon to kill a demon? Didn't I see you slaughtering souls with one?"

"I was the chief torturer in Hell once upon a time.

My blades only harm the dead. There are a few weapons to kill a demon, but the one at your hip is the only one on this plane, making it the only one I can get to."

"But why—"

Andras stands again, his power and rage growing, filling the room. This isn't the genial man I met just a few minutes ago, the one ready to tell his side. This is the man I expected him to be. "I've answered enough of your questions. Samael has already attacked me more than once. I need that blade. Give me what I asked for."

But he never asked, not really. He swindled, tricked, and threatened. He never asked me for help, only demanded. That's all he's ever done.

"No. And fun fact, that's the same answer I gave the Council when they asked me to kill you. Having this blade out in the open is just going to get people killed. You said it's the only one on this plane that can kill a demon, meaning he plans to steal it from you once you have it. I should lock this thing back up in the safe and drop it in the fucking ocean."

It's meant as a threat, and he takes it as such. His eyes glow bright, showing that underneath the man before me, he isn't much more than the devil I always assumed he was. Then I'm talking to no one, Andras disappears, reappearing behind Aidan, one hand on Aidan's chin, the other on the top of his head, ready to snap Aidan's neck. Aidan's a big man, but my father is bigger.

"No! Andras, what are you doing?" Teresa screams, disbelief in her every move. She didn't think he was capable of this.

Honestly? I didn't either. I also never expected the ripping of my heart when I see Aidan in danger, never thought I'd feel this weight of helplessness and dread. I've never had to protect him before, and I find the need of it more than I can bear.

"I will snap his neck like a twig, Maxima. You don't know me, but I know you. Being Rogue, you have so few friends, and this man is one of the only ones left standing. It won't hurt me to kill him. But it will hurt you. Give me the blade, and I'll let him go."

Aidan tries to wriggle in Andras' hold, but Andras only tightens his grip, hard enough for his talons to break skin on Aidan's neck, making him wince.

"Don't do it, Max. Don't you give him shit!" Aidan commands, and I want to do what he says.

I really want to, but I can't. My eyes trail over the blood dripping down his neck, back up to Aidan's pale-green eyes. He's always been the brave one. The stoic one. The one to show no fear.

But there's fear there now.

Andras tightens his grip again, and a pained gasp escapes Aidan's mouth. I don't expect the wet to hit my eyes, the fear dragging the tears from me against my will.

I pull the blade from the sheath Barrett spelled so only I could remove it, balancing the knife in my palm and hand it over. I don't spare Andras a glance. I'm still staring at Aidan as Andras lets his hold go lax to grab the blade. When the heat of Andras' gaze leaves my face, I do the only thing I can, I wink at Aidan. As luck would have it, he catches my hint, smoking out from Andras' grip, traveling out of danger and giving me just the diversion I need.

Reaching behind my back, I rip the athame from its sheath, slicing his arm just as his fingers close around the bone blade. What I'm not prepared for is the backhand that comes afterward. Andras has enough power in that single strike to knock me across the room and into a wall.

And then it's lights out.

My mother's concerned face is the absolute last one I thought I'd see.

"Maxima, honey, I need you to get up!" She shakes

my shoulders, her hands hard on what is likely a monster of a bruise.

"I'm up, I'm up." I groan, pushing myself up from my crumpled heap behind the love seat.

The room sways a bit and I blink once, hard, trying to reorder what I see now to the room it used to be. Honestly, it looks like a bomb hit it. The couch is a smoking ruin, the walls half-charred and still smoking. Aidan's nursing a bloody nose and a gash on his upper arm. Teresa's cheek is slightly burned, and she's holding her body just so, meaning her ribs are either bruised or broken.

"What the hell happened?" I ask, more to myself than anyone else because I can tell what happened. Andras kicked our ass, that's what happened.

"After Andras hit you, well... I got a little upset." There's the mother I know. Teresa Alcado has never been one to answer a direct question. "I might have set him on fire a little bit."

"I'll say. He got away, or am I going to find him vaporized under the couch?"

"He got away," Aidan answers from across the room. Oh, he's pissed, and I really hope it's not at me.

"Shit. What are the odds of him winning against Samael? Ball park?" I ask my mother, who probably knows what we're going up against better than either of us do.

Her wince is all the answer I need. Aces.

At just that second, someone pounds at the front door, and I've never prayed so hard that someone called the cops in my life, and I start to wonder where the hell my life went wrong that I'd hope it was a cop instead of another Ethereal. I stagger, pulling myself the rest of the way up, ready to fight if I need to. But when no one answers the door, a voice calls that I never expected to hear.

"Max, open the damn door!"

Striker. Then, I'm jumping over the tattered remnants of furniture and yanking open the door so fast it bangs against the wall and bounces back to knock me in the shoulder. Which hurts like a bitch.

Striker looks scruffy and worn, tired in a way only grief can accomplish. His blond mop of curls never looked so good, though, and soon I'm wrapped in the biggest bear hug ever. I didn't realize how much I missed the big lug.

"You sure know how to cause a ruckus, Maxie. I heard from a little bird you needed help."

"Gramma?" I wonder if his little bird is my grandmother.

"No, Maria. But I was already on the case. I've been

tracking the situation for some time—since a little after I left actually. Your family tree is a little fucked up, Princess."

Ugh. I hate that word. I'm a Rogue. I'm not princess of shit.

"Well, you're not wrong. Striker, you know Aidan, and this is my mother, Teresa."

Striker eyes her up and down like a snake about to strike, and my mother does the same, only one better.

"Which one of these men are you with, Maxima? Or are you creating a harem of men at your disposal?"

If only she knew my sex life has been as dry as the Sahara for what seems like years.

"Not to be a bitch or anything, but fuck you very much, Mother. Just because covens are usually all female doesn't mean I have to surround myself with a bunch of women. Just because that's how it's always been done doesn't mean that is the only way it can be done. I have friends who I don't sleep with who also come equipped with penises."

I turn to Striker. "Is it penises or penni?"

Striker chuckles. "Penises, sweet cheeks."

My mother looks like I just hit her in the face with a baseball bat. That'll teach her.

"You said you've been tracking the situation. Do you have any idea what's going on?" I ask Striker, because honestly, I have absolutely no idea who to trust. Do I trust Andras who has shown he would rather hurt me and mine to get what he needs?

"I've been tracking Samael. He is alive. Caim and a few of the others never believed he was really killed but needed to keep their reservations quiet. I've been following him for weeks. We're going to need that bone blade of yours if we want to stop him."

I huff out a sigh, perching on what's left of the couch. "That'll be a problem. Andras has the blade. Maybe we can go to Bernadette, see if maybe she can track it since she made the damn thing."

Striker shifts his feet, adjusting the collar of his shirt like he doesn't want to say what he's about to, but in true Striker fashion has to say the thing even if the thing is going to start some shit. "I wouldn't do that."

"Why not," my mother pipes in, finally over her shock of penis talk. "She would be one of the few who could track it."

Striker steps back, really looking at my mother. I see the debate warring behind his eyes. No one would know this but me, no one who hadn't known Striker as long as I had. He was questioning whether or not he could trust her. Whether or not she was worth his time or trust. "Because I just left Samael, and he was headed right for Bernadette. We can't trust her."

Aidan and I exchange a glance. In it is a single solitary thought. *Fuck.* Knowing what we know about Samael's plan, Striker has it wrong.

Bernadette isn't with Samael—I saw her face when she told me her son was dead. No one can fake that kind of grief. And if I know my father, he knows exactly where his brother is. With that Fates forsaken blade in his possession.

No. Bernadette isn't in league with Samael at all.

What she is, however, is a sitting duck.

21

MAX

"Where are Andras' weapons?" I ask my mother while searching the floor for mine. Aidan helps me move what's left of the couch where the athame seems to have escaped.

I remember dropping it when Micah nearly killed me, and I can only assume Aidan was the one to snag it for me. The sheath at my hip feels empty, and I realize I am the biggest idiot on the planet for handing the blade over to my father.

"I—I don't know."

"You mean to tell me you've been here for twenty-four hours, and you haven't searched the place yet?"

And then my eyes go wide as I catch her blush.

Teresa has been too busy diddling Dad to look too hard at her surroundings.

"You were hate-fucking your way through four hundred years of drama while my baby sister was bleeding to death in a damn closet, hiding from a Corax demon? What the fuck, Mother? Do you not give a shit about either one of your kids?" I didn't start that tirade yelling, but I damn well finish it that way.

My mother wrings her hands, staring at her feet instead of meeting my eyes. Shame. This is what shame looks like on my mother. I thought I'd never see the day.

"The demon attacked and Andras picked me up and got me out of there. I couldn't get to her in time and then when we were safe, I tracked her. I knew she was with you. I knew she was safe, and it wasn't like Andras was going to let me go anywhere."

"You didn't try to leave, did you? Your baby daddy broke through all my wards, leaving me defenseless while he delivered the message that he was holding you hostage. You weren't a hostage. You were a willing participant to his fuckery."

I swear to the Fates if she tells me she wasn't I will punch her right in the mouth.

"I don't have time for this. You are staying behind. Inform the Council of what we've learned. Make sure they know Samael is alive and is coming for them." I bang out the front door like my ass is on fire, Striker and Aidan at my heels. Dawn is fast approaching, and for some reason, the light on the horizon doesn't make me feel any better.

"Oh, and Mother? Say hi to Barrett for me," I toss over my shoulder. Let her make of that what she will.

I don't quite make it down the little sidewalk to the gate where the ward ends, before I slam into an invisible wall of magic that halts me before I can go anywhere. I know exactly what this is. This is Teresa Alcado not getting her way and throwing a temper tantrum.

I don't even turn around before the door opens, and my mother's voice whips the air behind me even though it is just over a whisper.

"I love you, Maxima, even if you think I don't." She huffs a breath before she begins speaking again, this time the words taking my breath away. "I bless you with all that I am, and all that I will be. May you have safety on your travels. May your aim always be true. May you see what others cannot. May your victories far outweigh your losses. May your losses teach you, and may your love guide you."

In her blessing, Teresa walks barefoot, circling us seven times. At the end, she slices her thumb with an athame, pressing the bloody digit into the skin of my chest just below my collar bone. I don't look but I sense she does the same to Striker and Aidan, blessing them just as she has me.

She stops right in front of me again, and it's then I notice my mother is far shorter than I am. She always seemed larger than life, but now I see her, really see her. She makes mistakes, she's stubborn, she does what she thinks is right even if it seems wrong. Ugh. We are more alike than I'd care to admit.

She presses her lips together so hard they turn white around the edges before she lets them go. "Be safe. Be smart. Survive. Understand?"

I blink through tears and nod. She presses the athame in my hand—the same one she used to cut her thumb—snaps her fingers, and then she's gone in a flash of red light. I glance down, noticing the athame looks a lot like the one in the sheath at my spine. Pulling mine free with trembling fingers, I compare them side by side.

They're identical.

The athame I've carried for years—through everything—has been my mother's all along.

"Am I hallucinating, or did your mother just do a nice thing?" Aidan asks behind me, lightly dropping a hand to my shoulder in comfort.

"I'd like to think it was a dream, but I'm not that lucky. Does this mean I have to start liking her now?" I'm joking, but only a little.

"Nah," Striker says, letting me off the hook.

I notice his Tesla parked at the curb. "You got anything decent in the trunk?" I point to the ostentatious vehicle. "I don't think a pair of athames are going to cut it."

"Oh, *sweetheart*." His grin turns positively evil. "Do I ever."

———

This time I don't make Aidan walk the two-point-three miles into the ass end of nowhere before the three of us travel into the valley, me on my own and Striker with Aidan, picking a spot further in the trees instead of out in the open near the stream. Unlike my usual reaction to wraith travel, Striker is no worse for wear. The fucker doesn't look even a little green, and I don't know if I should be irritated or proud.

Dawn is still a few hours off in central Colorado, and my eyesight isn't as acute as Aidan's, but I still catch the crouched, malformed demons lurking in a perfect circle around Bernadette's cabin just outside her ward.

My breath catches as I grip Aidan's wrist. "Can you see them?" I murmur, trying not to move, not to breathe. Corax demons are invisible to most Ethereals, and I don't know if my mother's blessing helped the boys see what they normally wouldn't.

"Yes. This was the thing you sent us away to fight on your own? I ought to tan your ass for letting us leave you like that."

I peel my eyes from the dozen Corax demons just chilling, waiting for us to arrive to ring the dinner bell, to check if Aidan's serious.

He is. He so is. His green eyes flash with indignation and something else. Something I can't place. Not fear, not anger. I don't know *what* it is.

"You should have left with us," he growls, his eyes flashing wraith black.

Honestly, he's probably right, but I can't change the past.

"At least I'm not heading into this fray by myself?" I whisper, wincing, trying not to shrug it off. Aidan looks like he might wrap me in bubble wrap and mail me home if I do that.

Striker sidles up beside me. "What do you think? Knock-out spell? Slowing spell? Any fucking spell that makes us not those monsters' dinner, I'm all for it."

"It's not like I can just pull a spell out of my ass," I whisper-hiss, trying not to alert the gigantic scary monsters that torture people in Hell for a living that we're there. "I need their blood, tissue, something."

Hang on. I stabbed one through the skull with my athame. I don't know if I killed it true dead, but that isn't the point. I might still have some blood on the blade. I yank the athame free, pressing the rune to expand the blade.

There.

In a groove that runs the length of the top of the blade is a long black streak. Corax blood.

I examine the blade. "Never mind. I have some." Reaching into the pack of witchy supplies Striker had in his car—bless him—I pull a vial of salt. Maria can have all the ingredients in her spells if she wants to, but nothing beats raw power, fire, and salt.

"I don't have enough blood to knock them all out, but I can slow them down."

I murmur words I'd used on another demon not too long ago, slowing his magic to a crawl, and this time, I'm not wounded. Drawing a circle of salt, I snap my fingers, letting the flame of my magic rise in my hand. Muttering the words, I let the flame of my magic heat the blade.

Subsisto, tardo, confuto, concesso, subflamino, insisto, conquiesco, finis.

I pour salt over the tang of the blade, letting the granules stick to the thick, tar-like blood.

Subsisto, tardo, confuto, concesso, subflamino, insisto, conquiesco, finis.

Passing the flame of the blade again, the blood bubbles, boiling until there is nothing left.

Smiling, I peer around Aidan's bulk, spying on the big malformed barriers between us and the cabin. One of them staggers.

Yep, it's working.

"I don't know how long we have, so be quick. Beheadings are hard to come back from, trust me, so go with that. Also, Striker, you may want to phase," I suggest, remembering the thick hide of scales that covered his arms the last time he sprouted wings. "Those talons are sharp."

At my statement, Aidan lets out a slow, building growl as he yanks a thick sword from the scabbard at his back. *Okay...* Someone is cranky.

Edging closer to the end of the tree line, I keep a close eye on the Corax, making sure the spell actually took. The demons stumble on nothing, each one finding their knees in the dirt.

Then everything goes straight to Hell.

As soon as we reach the stream, a falcon screams, taking flight from a low branch, circling the demons, the piercing shriek waking them from their induced stupor. One by one, their plucked raven heads turn right to us.

I've never wanted to murder an animal out of spite before, but today is that day. But then I recognize that fucking bird. It was on my street when Ian was kidnapped. I saw it the last time I came to Bernadette's. Hell, I even heard a bird's shriek when I was bloody and broken after the last time I tangled with a Corax.

That isn't a bird. It's a spy.

"Go! Take the demons out. I've got the bird."

Breaking off into a run, I reach for the bag of spelled rocks Maria gave me. I'd scoffed at the time, but beaning one of these motherfuckers against that damn bird's skull is going to be fucking glorious.

My feet are sure on the uneven ground despite my choice of shoes, and my mind falls to my mother's blessing. *I really hope Mom laid a good whammy on me,* I think as I pull a red agate from my pouch and gear up for a toss. The falcon is perched in an Aspen, the fluttery green leaves, half-concealing it, but still I let the rock fly.

The red ones are powered with a disabling spell. Meant for small things like guard dogs. Don't try it on powerful Ethereals. It'll just piss them off.

That's when I stopped listening to Maria, but dammit if she didn't come through in a clutch because the rock hits the bird right in the chest, knocking it from the tree. It falls, landing in the dirt in a great puff of dust, unmoving.

Thanks, little sister.

"*Ipsum revelare.*" I snap my fingers at the unconscious animal, praying I'm wrong. *Reveal yourself.*

If it's a shifter of some kind, I want to know. I want to know if a sentient being that knows right and wrong just sold us—sold me—out. I want to know if it's who I think it is.

The transformation is slow, but that's expected. I'm forcing a shifter to change at dawn, my magic going against their very nature, but feathers soon fall away, and flesh grows in their stead—the phase back to human-shaped, crumbling my sister's spell to dust.

But the bird is exactly who I thought it would be.

When the blonde stands before me it is all I can do not to drive my athame right into her skull.

"Hiya, Ruby. Having a rough day?"

22

MAX

I don't know at what point I wanted to be wrong about Ruby, but the betrayal coursing through my veins takes me by surprise. I still remember the woman who pulled me aside and told me where to go for help when she saw my brands. I remember the woman who found out how I was named Rogue and commiserated with me.

Then I realize, I'm looking at a completely different woman than the one who faked her way through our meeting at Caim's. The woman before me now is a rage-filled shell of the woman I met those few weeks ago. Micah's words fill my brain.

You think I'm the only one who wants you to burn? That blonde bitch who sent me after you? She's watching you. Always watching you.

I'd thought he was lying, but he wasn't at all.

Micah was a murdering psychopath, but he wasn't lying. Not about this.

Ruby's blonde hair falls down into two disheveled plaits, dressed in now-dirt-covered jeans and boots, she seems almost normal outside of Caim's club. Wholesome. And the disparity between what she looks like and what she is almost kills me. Ruby has always used her looks like a weapon, and as bitchy as she is, I never expected this from her.

She doesn't even appear sorry, the delicate jut of her chin turning mulish in her silence.

"I could make you tell me why, but I'd rather you offer it freely. How could you do this?" My voice breaks on my whisper.

But Ruby doesn't heed my warning, she begins her phase, bones cracking, her spine bowing with the strain. I don't wait for her to strike.

"*Constringitur in locum.*" I freeze her where she stands, the spell halting her mid-transformation, the angel wings I expected to see budding from her back like flowers about to open.

"I can't hurt you because of what you are, even though you hurt me. But I'll make sure Caim knows about this. I'll make sure Barrett and Marcus and Gorgon and Cinder know about it, too," I threaten, and then turn my back on her, not sparing her another glance. I've got bigger problems at the moment than a bitchy half-breed angel.

Corax demons swarm the entry point to my grandmother's cabin, clashing with Aidan and Striker. Striker is phased into his other form, a mix of angel and whatever the hell he's mixed with. Given the scales—and the knowledge that they actually fucking exist—I'd go with dragon. He has come into his other form, wielding the half-feathered, half-scaled wings like extensions of himself, using them to strike the Corax before he takes their head.

Aidan's fighting style is less flashy, and more about stealth. Using his abilities, he slides in and out of sight, popping behind demons only to take their heads and popping back out again.

About a half dozen lay in the dirt missing their heads, but the rest are staying just outside the warding lines as if they can see them, fending off Aidan and Striker less like they want to kill them, and more like they are just fodder for keeping them out of Bernadette's home. I can't imagine what would happen to the Corax if they touched the pale luminescent hex lines of Bernadette's ward, and at that thought, an idea forms at the same time a smile stretches my lips wide.

Instead of wasting my time by running, I snap my

fingers, traveling from the rocky shore of the stream to the demon unfortunate enough to be closest to the hex lines. Catching him by surprise, his talons flail, bird eyes going wide as I drive my athame-turned-sword into its chest. The demon falls, lighting up like a Christmas tree against the ward before he explodes in a spray of demon guts and sludge I only manage to avoid by an inch.

The smell—*Fates, I forgot about the smell*—is enough to make me gag. The stench of rot nearly bowls me over, which is why the demon's buddy catches me by surprise. So much for Aidan's lessons on situational awareness. Talons catch me at the shoulder, ripping an agony-inducing swath down my back.

Blood pours from the wounds I'm probably glad I can't see, driving me to my knees. Then a bird head falls to the ground independent from the humanish body it was previously attached to. A hand appears in front of my face, and I lever myself up off the ground with it, the bulk of the heavy lifting done by the man attached to it.

"Remind me to re-teach you how to *not* be snuck up on in our next lesson," Aidan quips, not quite able to mask the concern leaking into his tone.

"I'll get right on that." I try not to hurl at the agony filling me.

Then I move, or should I say, Aidan moves me.

Curling me around his back, he parries with another demon's talons, fighting off strike after strike. But this demon isn't alone. No, this motherfucker brought friends. Two more Corax head for us, the pair of them galloping on their hooves faster than any horse.

Pulling deep, I flex my magics. Breathing on my fingers, I let the spell weave through me, letting the power build. I can almost see the striations of gold in their black beady eyes before I let my fingers loose, the magic snapping like a rubber band through me and outward. The spell circles them in a shower of green magic, whipping the pair of demons up and away, into the hex lines of the ward.

The pair of them look like mosquitos on a bug zapper before they go boom, sending black, tar-like blood and sludge raining over us.

"For Fates sake, Maxima, was that really necessary?" Striker yells while taking the last demon's head. I can't blame him. He and Aidan caught the brunt of the spray, being so tall. Striker most of all since his wingspan is a greater surface area.

"Three were attacking at once. I was helping!" I yell back, only slightly sorry for dousing us all in demon guts.

Aidan stares down at me where I wilted once the

spell left my fingers, black sludge covering his beanie and half his face. "Don't help anymore, okay?"

"Fine. Next time you can take on three Corax demons at once by yourself." I huff, trying to ignore the pulsing torment also known as my back.

I try to stand, the ground shifting beneath my feet, and at first, I think it's just me. Just the blood loss making my legs shaky, but Aidan throws a hand out for balance, too. A rumble from inside the ward grows, spilling out through the hex lines so much, the light of them bends with the strain.

Then the world goes white, the blast of the ward breaking sending us flying, careening into the stream. The water hitting my face is a shock, and I try to claw my way to the surface, but there is a weight on my back holding me down. Pushing as hard as I can, I scrabble my way to the surface, breathing fresh air in what feels like too long. I discover the weight on me isn't something I can just throw off. It's Aidan's limp body that must have taken the brunt of the blast. I feel him breathing, feel his heartbeat through the fabric of my shirt.

Thank the Fates.

Letting him rest on my back, I pull my knees under me, dragging him along with me as I yank us both out of the water. Once the sand sifts through my fingers, I shrug him off, letting him hit the ground as I catch my breath for a second before checking him over. Other than the goose egg that he will definitely feel later, he seems fine.

I search for Striker, finding him on the bank of the stream, his head still in the water. I manage to pull his heavy ass to the bank and make sure he's actually breathing. Luckily, only his hair was in the water. One thing I can say for our impromptu bath, at least it washed some of the demon guts off me.

Turning, I look back at my grandmother's cabin, the ward now a gaping hole of dissipating magic, and grasp just why the ward blew in the first place. Souls swarm the cabin, gray and black trails of smoke and darkness. Their screams are piercing even from this far away.

Aidan said they were drawn to the blade. That means Andras is here.

Samael's here.

Grandma's here.

Might as well make it a family reunion.

Walking through the spirits, I marvel at how they don't even look at me. Since I don't have the blade, they aren't even remotely interested in me—just the way I like it. Ghost problems are bullshit.

My entry into Bernadette's cabin goes mostly unnoticed. Spirits swirl inside the walls, the bulk of them inside rather than out. Bernadette is on the floor, the bone blade protruding from the meat of her shoulder. My father and uncle clash in the kitchen, the pair of them with bone swords that had to come from a giant or a dragon or something. I've never seen either up close, but nothing human sized could produce a bone that big. My uncle appears similar to my father. The same dark hair, same nose, same glowing gold eyes.

But that's where the similarities end. Samael is dressed in a dark suit, fighting with precision and class like a champion fencer. Andras is in jeans and a flannel, fighting like a bare-knuckles backroom brawler. Either way, neither one is winning.

The specters hover over Bernadette, slashing at her with hands I know are so cold they burn. Her skin is black in some places where the cold is so bad it's decayed the flesh, and for the first time, I see her other form. She fades in and out of the cultured but aging lady to a beautiful raven-haired young woman, her face so beautiful it almost hurts to look at her.

Sliding next to her, I reach for the blade, ready to pull it from her shoulder, but she stops me.

"No, Maxima." Her breaths are fast and labored as if it's taking everything she has in her to stay conscious, to stay sane. "Do-don't take it. The spirits, the-they'll kill you. They're dr-drawn to the blade."

Meeting her eyes, her pain brims from her every pore. "I know. Samael put that there?" I ask, drawing the blade from her flesh.

She nods, her eyes filling. "Andras saved me. I never should have doubted him."

I can only nod. She might be able to trust my father, but I sure as fuck can't. "I'll take care of it."

As soon as the blade is free, the spirits swarm me, their hands cutting into my flesh, the cold stealing my breath. But I've thought of the only way to stop them.

They have to go back where they came from.

"*Veni in domum suam, vacui hoc imple. Reperio tenebrae tuae in hoc loco.*" The spell is simple, the words flowing from my tongue as if someone planted them there. *Come home, fill this void. Find your place in this darkness.*

The souls howl, blowing apart before swirling faster, harder, tighter against me, ripping into my flesh with cold fingers. They draw blood, they burn me.

Veni in domum suam, vacui hoc imple. Reperio tenebrae tuae in hoc loco.

A soul solidifies in front of me—a young woman cut down too soon. She screams in my face, wrapping a freezing hand around my throat, squeezing, stealing all my air. They don't want to go, but there is nowhere else. Stuck between planes, stuck between worlds, left to rot in a cage they were never meant for but can't escape.

Bernadette grabs my hand, repeating my words, lending me her voice when mine is gone, lending me eons worth of power to draw from.

Veni in domum suam, vacui hoc imple. Reperio tenebrae tuae in hoc loco.

Then the hand at my throat is gone, the soul tugged back by an invisible thread, they swirl closer to the blade, the power in the blade growing as souls start to fill it.

"Now, Maxima. Give me the blade!" Andras screams, his arms wrapped around Samael's chest and neck, holding my struggling uncle in place.

I don't need to even consider it to know Andras can't be trusted, so I don't give the blade to him. Instead, I let the dagger fly, throwing it with all my strength and pray that my mother's blessing holds steadfast.

May your aim always be true.

Watching as the tang turns over and over in the air, I feel the souls drawing away from me. Feel them follow the blade, feel them fill it with the power of hundreds, thousands of deaths. The point of the dagger pierces Samael's heart, the weight of the power driving the blade home.

He stops struggling, his body wilting in Andras' hold. Andras lets his brother slide to the floor, and I stagger to my kill, yanking the dagger free once the last of Samael's breath leaves him.

I stare at the bone. That's all it is. Just a bone from some creature filed down into the most basic of weapons. What once held something full of life, now takes it without compunction.

This doesn't need to be here.

"No one needs this blade. No one needs this kind of power," I croak, my voice a bitter husk of breath.

The power I shied away from fills my hand as I stare at my grandmother, her form once again the aging beauty. "I know you wanted it for a rainy day, but you'll just have to keep on living a while longer."

A ghost of a smile flits across her lips, and she gives me a subtle nod. I don't bother looking at my father as he stands staring at me as if he's never seen me before. I suppose he hasn't.

The old Max wouldn't have to step between two family members.

The old Max didn't have a family.

But I suppose he never knew the old Max, either.

I draw some of the magic into me—just enough to do what I need to. Then using that little bit, I grip the bone, tossing the magics back into it, overloading it, cracking it, crushing the blade until it's nothing more than bone shards and dust in my hand.

Then, and only then, do I look at my father. I hold my hand out to him, but he doesn't take the bait.

I sprinkle the floor with the bone dust. "Here's your blade, Father."

I hope you choke on it, I think, walking out of the cabin into the sunshine.

23

MAX

Barrett stares me down as I sit right back where I started in a velvet green armchair in the middle of the high court room. At least this time when I was escorted to the witch club, Aether, by an Ethereal Guard, Ruby wasn't the one to have her mitts on me. No, that was reserved for the twenty or so witches, angels, shifters, and even a few *no shit* dragons waiting for me when I strolled —okay, hobbled—out of Bernadette's cabin. The cavalry had arrived, even if they were about an hour too late and lost Ruby in the shuffle.

At least Mother actually listened to me.

"You're telling me you killed Samael, didn't kill Andras like you were supposed to, put a freezing spell on an angel, and destroyed the bone blade." He checks the facts of my story, making sure he has them all.

"Yep." I cross my feet on the matching ottoman I conjured for my own personal comfort. Hell, I was bleeding, covered in Corax guts—*still*—and I was pretty sure I was half-delirious. Barrett could ask me if I killed the Queen of England, and I'd probably answer the same, but at least he's keeping to relevant topics.

Aidan and Striker were whisked in and out of here with a pat on the head and a "good job," but not me.

Nooooooo...

I was stuck getting the evil eye from a man who might like me, might respect me, but also might kill me if the need arose. I was too tired to give him any more details. Personally, I was hoping Bernadette would swoop in and save me from the interrogation brewing behind his eyes.

I need a medic.

And a bottle of bourbon.

Preferably not in that order.

"Do you care that Samael wasn't actually murdered by Andras, Ruby was a spy for Samael, and the bone blade was going to cause the Apocalypse? Because I feel those are all important facts to remember here."

"And we should believe you, why exactly?" Barrett asks, the snideness slipping heavily in his tone.

"Knock it off. Can't you see she's bleeding all over the place?" Marcus comes to my rescue, and I kinda want to hug the shifter. I also kinda want to sleep for a week, so hugging is probably out.

Barrett smiles at his mate. "Fine. Ruin my payback for the door incident why don't you."

"What door incident?" Caim leans around Cinder and Gorgon, the gaping hole of the demon seat only highlighting my grandmother's absence. If Caim was surprised Ruby was working for the other side, he didn't show it. But then again, he was one of the few who sent Striker off on his mission, so he might have already known how treacherous she could be.

"Max blew up that door," Barrett says almost proudly, pointing to the entrance to the high court room, "like it was nothing, and then *poof*, put the damn thing back together again like she never blew it to smithereens in the first bloody place. We need to talk to your Fae builder. If that thing can be blown apart by a bloody child, we're all in trouble."

"Oh, give it a rest. I'm fucking bleeding over here. I know I'm not in trouble. You know I'm not in trouble. Just give me my damn cookie for saving the world as we know it *again* and let me get stitched up," I gripe, ready to blow up that stupid door again.

And this time I won't put it back together, either.

"As you wish," Barrett murmurs, breathing on his fingers before rubbing them together.

Heat washes over me, stealing the bitter cold still lingering on my skin from the spirits who attacked so mercilessly. It steals away the ache in my back, the burning agony of the open wounds. I feel it knit my flesh back together, feel the power of Barrett's magic heal me, finally breathing easy for the first time in what feels like a week.

"Thank you," I breathe, wilting into the chair.

"I was wondering when you'd snap. You lasted far longer than I thought you would," Barrett says, a laugh not quite breaking free. "Maxima Alcado, born Maxima Christina Arcadios, former member of the now-defunct Arcadios Coven, daughter of the demon Andras and Pacific Northwest coven leader, Teresa Alcado, sole heir to the royal seat, your Rogue status is hereby rescinded. Any action against you is now considered a direct threat to the Council and will be dealt with as such."

Barrett pauses, likely letting me digest this new information. *Your Rogue status is hereby rescinded.* How long have I wanted to hear those words? Forever, maybe? And yet, they don't feel real. Like this is some sort of trick, some sort of treachery just winding up for the pitch. Shaking, I can barely blink, barely breathe.

"We offer you the vacant demon seat, child. We offer you what should have always been yours." My eyes stray from Barrett to Gorgon, the warlock's kind pronouncement hitting me square in the chest.

If this is a trick, Gorgon isn't part of it, but I know what too good to be true looks like. I've seen it more than once.

Too good to be true is me getting sent to kill one man, when another is responsible. It's me being turned Rogue in the first place. It's the maneuvering and politicking. It's the vagueness, the half-told truths and the bold-faced lies.

"Will anyone be offended if I say I'll think about it? While I appreciate my status as Rogue being rescinded, the Council seat is a very important job—one I'm not sure I'm ready for," I say as diplomatically as I possibly can. Actually, I'm quite proud of myself.

"Don't tarry too long," Barrett advises. "And keep a watchful eye on your assistant. Vampires are nearly extinct, you know."

Barrett drops that bomb, and then just like that, I'm dismissed to digest the mythical fucking creature on my payroll.

Thanks, Gramma.

Walking out the high court room into Aether proper, I spot Striker in a seat on the outskirts of the club. Even in the middle of the day, the place is packed, and I can't quite figure out if these people have jobs or lives. It all feels artificial and weird like most clubs do once the shine wears off.

"Let me guess, you're here for the food."

Striker startles and then turns his head, looking away from the naked acrobats and topless bartenders, away from the nakedness and fun. "Just enjoying the entertainment, boss."

Everything from the slope of his shoulders, to his voice, to the way his eyes seem a little lost tell me his grief over Melody's death isn't gone—not by a long shot. But I don't know what to do for my friend. Being in the human world didn't help, and even here—in this fake, superficial place —filled with glamours and flesh and magic and sex, he seems better than he was. Even if it's only a little bit.

Maybe he needs the superficial right now.

"Yeah, well, I'm going home. Don't stay too long. Too much of this place will rot your brain," I warn. As if it will do any good, as if he'll even listen to me.

I leave him behind, finding the door and getting the hell out of this place. Leaning against the glamoured warehouse wall, Aidan lounges, his feet crossed at the ankle, his face turned up to the sun. I'm half-tempted to leave him there, he looks so peaceful.

"You waiting on me?"

One of Aidan's eyes slowly opens, giving me the

perfect side-eye for a man who probably has a concussion. "No, I'm waiting on some other chick. Tell me when you see her, she's hard to miss. She's about yay high, blue hair, covered in demon guts." He gives me a crooked little smile. "They throw the book at you?"

"Nah. Just got my Rogue status revoked is all." I smile as I turn and start walking toward the right side of town—where people and coffee reside—leaving Aidan to trail after me.

I showered until all the hot water ran out. Then I called Della for the first time since my shop burned down. Turns out that while Bernadette was a little lax on who she sent to watch out for me, Della's benefits far outweighed any downsides.

Della was a little vague on the details, but the human side of my building being burned down was taken care of. I don't know how, but every single customer thinks they weren't there that day, or in Della-speak: "I handled it, boss."

And the building? Well, the repairs were already under way. I wasn't sure I wanted to ask questions, so I didn't.

Some things I just don't need to know. So I have a

vampire on staff who can walk in the sun? I'm a demon-witch hybrid who seems to be the only one of my kind.

Who am I to judge?

In fact, the only person I am fit to judge is Ruby, and I'm going to find her feathery ass if it's the last thing I do.

Apocalypse be damned.

Max's story will continue with
Lady of Madness & Moonlight
Rogue Ethereal Book Three

LADY OF MADNESS & MOONLIGHT
Rogue Ethereal Book Three

A former Rogue being presented to the Fates. What could go wrong?

When I was offered a seat on the Ethereal Council, no one said anything about meeting the actual Fates. On the day of my presentation, not only do I offend the three women who control every single thread of life, but an Angel's thread is cut short, and no one knows how.

Now it's my job to find out who did it before the death gets pinned on me and starts an all-out Angel-Demon war.

Maybe being a Rogue was the least of my problems.

Grab Lady of Madness & Moonlight Today!

DEAD TO ME

Grave Talker Book One

Meet Darby. Coffee addict. Homicide detective. Oh, and she can see ghosts, too.

There are only three rules in Darby Adler's life.
One: Don't talk to the dead in front of the living.
Two: Stay off the Arcane Bureau of Investigation's radar.
Three: Don't forget rules one and two.

With a murderer desperate for Darby's attention and an

ABI agent in town, things are about to get mighty interesting in Haunted Peak, TN.

Grab Dead to Me today!

THE PHOENIX RISING SERIES

an adult paranormal romance series by Annie Anderson

Heaven, Hell, and everything in between. Fall into the realm of Phoenixes and Wraiths who guard the gates of the beyond. That is, if they can survive that long...

Living forever isn't all it's cracked up to be.

Check out the Phoenix Rising Series today!

JOIN THE LEGION

EXCLUSIVE SNEAK PEEKS,
GIVEAWAYS, BOOK DISCUSSION.
COME FOR THE BOOKS.
STAY FOR THE MEMES.

To stay up to date on all things Annie Anderson, get exclusive access to ARCs and giveaways, and be a member of a fun, positive, drama-free space, join The Legion!

ABOUT THE AUTHOR

 Annie Anderson is the author of the international bestselling Rogue Ethereal series. A United States Air Force veteran, Annie pens fast-paced Urban Fantasy novels filled with strong, snarky heroines and a boatload of magic. When she takes a break from writing, she can be found binge-watching The Magicians, flirting with her husband, wrangling children, or bribing her cantankerous dogs to go on a walk.

To find out more about Annie and her books, visit
www.annieande.com

www.ingramcontent.com/pod-product-compliance
Lightning Source LLC
Chambersburg PA
CBHW050246110726
47898CB00007B/2294